THE BOYS START THE WAR

Phyllis Reynolds Naylor

A YEARLING BOOK

To the young readers of Buckhannon, West Virginia,
which is almost, but not quite,
the location of this story.

Published by
Bantam Doubleday Dell Books for Young Readers
a division of
Bantam Doubleday Dell Publishing Group, Inc.
1540 Broadway
New York, New York 10036

ISBN: 0-440-40971-3

Reprinted by arrangement with Delacorte Press

Printed in the United States of America

July 1994

10 9 8 7 6 5 4 3

OPM

Contents

One

The Aliens

"The island's sinking!"

Wally studied the rivers of yellow that began streaming out from the middle.

"Sandbags! Sandbags!" he cried, lifting his waffle up at the edges with his fork, first one side, then the other.

If he made a little cut in each corner, the hot syrup traveled from one square to the next, but if he poured the syrup directly over the pat of butter, sitting like an island in the middle of his breakfast, the island grew smaller and smaller as the butter melted, until finally . . .

"They're coming!"

The back door banged and Wally jumped. Jake and Josh came tumbling into the kitchen, followed by seven-year-old Peter.

"Who?" asked Wally.

"The new guys over in Bensons' house!" Jake

grabbed the field glasses from the shelf where Mother kept them after she finished her bird-watching. "C'*mon*!"

Feet pounded on the stairs, and Wally knew that his brothers were headed for the trapdoor in the attic ceiling and the small balcony on top of the house—the widow's walk, it was called—where they could see out over the whole town, practically.

He sighed, picked up his plate and fork, and went up the first flight of stairs to the bedrooms, then the second set of stairs to the attic.

He could never understand why his two older brothers were always in such a rush. Sooner or later they would find out whether the three new boys in that family were their own ages or not, so why the hurry? Wally felt that you should spend the last week of summer vacation as lazily as possible, and now he couldn't even enjoy his waffle in peace.

Yesterday Josh had been sitting under a tree sketching Martians, or what he thought Martians would look like. Jake had been figuring out what they would all do on Halloween, and Wally and Peter had been lying in the grass, watching ants crawling in and out of a rotten apple—exactly the kinds of ways you expected to spend a summer day. Peter was the only one in the family who liked to study things the way Wally did. They both had brown hair, blue eyes, and thick, sturdy hands like their father's. Jake and Josh, however, were string-bean skinny, with skin that tanned by the first week of June.

THE BOYS START THE WAR

Jake already had the stepladder in place, and Josh climbed to the top and pushed up on the trapdoor. Blue sky shone through the square opening as a shower of pigeon droppings rained down on them. One piece landed on Wally's waffle. One gray-white blob of digested worms and bugs. Wally stared helplessly at his plate, then set it on the floor and followed his brothers to the balcony above.

He sat down in one corner and watched as Jake inched forward on his stomach, field glasses in hand, until he was close to the railing. The wind whipped at Wally's shirt, but it was a warm, dry wind that spelled September.

"Why are they just sitting there?" Jake wondered aloud, holding the glasses steady as he stared across the river.

Wally squinted, studying the car in the driveway of the house at the end of Island Avenue. The large piece of land in the middle of Buckman was not really an island, because water surrounded only three sides of it, but people called it "The Island" anyway. If you were coming in from the east, you entered Buckman on Island Avenue and kept going until you were out on the very tip, and then you crossed the bridge over into the business district. You might not even have noticed that the river on your right was the same as that on your left; it simply looped about at the end of the island.

"Okay, a door's opening, here they come!" said Jake.

"How old are they?" Josh asked.

Wally hoped there would be friends for each of them—an eleven-year-old for the twins, a nine-year-old for him, and a seven-year-old friend for Peter. The family that had moved out of the house on the other side of the river—who had left West Virginia to go to Georgia—had five boys of all ages, and they had been the best friends the Hatfords ever had.

"Well, say something!" demanded Peter when Jake didn't answer. "Are they aliens or what?"

"There's the father," said Jake. "Now someone's getting out one of the back doors. . . . A guy about twelve, I'd guess. . . ."

"Yea!" cheered Josh.

"No, wait a minute . . . it's a girl . . . no, a boy. . . ." Jake's voice began to fade. "A girl. She just took off her cap."

A girl! Wally and Josh stared at each other. Who said anything about girls?

Josh took the field glasses next. He sat with his elbows propped on his knees, staring across the river. "No one else is getting out. . . . Now the other door's opening. It's the mother. . . . Here come the rest." He gasped. "Another girl . . . !"

"*Two* girls?" wailed Jake.

Wally thoughtfully bit his lip. This *was* serious! He grabbed the field glasses himself. "My turn," he said.

At the tip of the island a man and woman stood looking up at a large old house. Wally could see a tall girl behind them, leaning against a tree and holding a baseball cap in one hand. A smaller girl was running down to the river.

Another leg emerged from the backseat of the car. A sneakered foot, faded jeans, a knee, a thigh, and then the last member of the new family got out and stretched.

"A girl," said Wally, disbelieving, and handed the field glasses back to Josh.

Nobody spoke for almost a minute.

"They're aliens, all right," said Josh.

"Three kids in one family and they're all girls?" Jake cried incredulously. "I thought Mrs. Benson told Mom they had rented their house to a family with three boys!"

Wally tried to remember exactly. "She said she thought there were three kids—"

"And that maybe we would still have enough to play baseball. . . ." added Josh. "*I* thought she meant *boys*!"

Wally's shoulders slumped. For years, ever since he could remember, the Hatford and Benson boys had got together every afternoon, rain or shine, to shoot BBs, fish, swim, play kick-the-can, camp out near Smuggler's Cove, climb Knob Hill, explore the old coal mine, or just lie on their backs in the grass and talk.

More than that, with the five Benson boys, the Hatford brothers regularly won first place in the costume contest at Halloween. One year they had each dressed up like some of the teachers at school; another year they had been dominoes; and a third year they chained themselves together like a prison gang. With the nine of them they had their own baseball team, and every May played a team from Grafton. They had even started their own band. Nothing would be the same again.

Wally stared out over the hills that dipped and rose like a roller coaster all around Buckman. The steeples of the United Methodist Church and the college chapel peeped up over the tops of the trees surrounding the courthouse, and the shiny horse-shoe of a river curved around the island. It was a wonderful old town, but anytime he and his brothers walked over the swinging footbridge now, they would find three girls in the last house on Island Avenue, not the friends they had known all their lives.

"We just figured it would be a family of boys, that's all," he said at last.

"Well, we figured wrong," said Josh.

For a long while there was not another sound from the widow's walk. Finally Jake broke the silence:

"Let's burn the bridge."

Wally turned and stared. "What?"

"Just go down there some night and burn the footbridge," Jake said. "Then the girls couldn't get over to our side of the river. Not here, anyway.

They'd have to cross the road bridge and get to school the long way around."

"Don't be dumb," said Josh. "Dad would kill us."

"We don't have to burn the bridge. We'll just never invite them over here," said Wally.

"That's not enough," said Jake.

"We won't have anything to do with them," offered his twin, whose arms and legs were as long and spidery as Jake's.

"Not enough," said Jake.

"Well, what *do* you want to do, then? Vaporize them?" asked Peter, getting right to the point.

Jake sat with his lips pressed hard together and Wally could almost see currents connecting in his brain. Jake was the ringleader, the planner, and he usually got his way. "Do you remember the movie we saw once, *The Gang from Reno*?"

"Yeah," said Josh and Wally.

"No," said Peter.

"It was about this village up in the mountains," Jake told him. "A motorcycle gang from Reno comes and takes over. But the villagers finally drive them out just by making them miserable. We've got to make the new people miserable."

Wally leaned against the railing and studied Jake. It sounded pretty awful, even talking about it. "How do you know that the Bensons will move back if we do?"

"Because they weren't sure they'd like Georgia,

so they're only renting out their house here instead of selling. If they have trouble keeping renters, they just might give up and move back. You *know* they'd really rather live here. *Any*body would rather live here. We're just helping them make up their minds, that's all."

"But how are we going to make the new family miserable?" asked Josh, and they all turned to Wally. This always happened. Wally got involved whether he wanted to or not. He always said the first thing that came to his head, and that's why his brothers asked him.

"*Think,* Wally!" said Jake. "Think of the most terrible, awful, disgusting, horrible thing in the world."

Wally tried. He wondered if there was anything more awful or disgusting than pigeon poop on a waffle.

"Dead fish," he said finally.

Jake and Josh looked at each other.

"That's it!" yelped Josh. "We could dump them on the bank over on the other side, and the family will think the river's polluted."

"We'll dump everything dead we can find, and they'll be afraid to swim or fish or anything," said Jake. "Start collecting all the dead stuff you can, and put it in a bag in the garage. Great idea, Wally!"

"Hoo boy!" cried Josh. "The war is on!"

"Wow!" said Peter.

Wally blinked. How had this happened? What

had become of his wonderful day? Only a few minutes ago he'd been peacefully planning to float a waffle box down the river—see if it would make the curve at the end of Island Avenue and come back up the other side. Then he was going to climb to the top of the courthouse to see if there really were bats up there, the way Josh said, and after that he was going to jump from the largest branch of the sycamore into the river, and maybe he would even have gone out to the cemetery after dark, just to say he'd been.

He waited his turn at the trapdoor and slowly climbed down the ladder to the attic below. He picked up his plate, went down to the kitchen, scrunched up the empty waffle box and his waffle along with it, and then, with a sigh, threw them both in the trash.

Two

Burial at Sea

Caroline Malloy leapt out of the car and rushed across the lawn, her ponytail flying out behind her like a flag.

"The river!" she screeched. "Beth! Eddie! Look!"

Edith Ann, the oldest, who hated her name and made everyone call her Eddie, stuck her baseball cap back on her head and wandered over. Beth, who had had her nose in a book, *The Living Tentacles of Planet Z,* ever since the family left Ohio that morning, came slowly across the yard, turning a page as she walked, and probably would have stepped right off the edge of the bank if Caroline hadn't caught her.

"Look!" Caroline said again, and the three sisters stared out over the Buckman River.

They were lined up like steps. Eddie, eleven, was tallest by far, and always wore her cap, even to the dinner table. Beth, ten, was fair-haired and pale-skinned, and tended to list to one side in a strong wind. It was eight-year-old Caroline, with dark hair and eyes like her father's, who had big plans for that river. Caroline, her mother always said, was precocious.

"I hope there are rapids!" she cried. "I hope there's a dam and a waterfall and quicksand and snakes . . ."

She couldn't go on. It was just too exciting. If they were only going to be here a year, she wanted to make the most of it. Caroline wanted to be an actress, and she imagined a scene in which she was floating unconscious in the water, heading for the falls, and someone had to rescue her. Or she might be sinking in quicksand, and would cleverly grab a vine at the last minute to pull herself out.

If it was a really dangerous scene where she had to paddle through rapids or something, she could always count on Eddie to be her stuntwoman. In fact, if Eddie did the hard parts and Beth wrote the script, the three of them could play almost any scene they liked.

They'd call their company Malloy Studios, her dream went on, and it would take its place beside Universal and Paramount in Hollywood. Actress, scriptwriter, and stuntwoman, all related. Not that Beth and Eddie knew anything about this, of course.

"Caroline on the River," she said to the others. "Would that make a good movie title, Beth?"

"*The River on Caroline*, maybe," Eddie told her.

Beth made a face. "Movie titles have to be mysterious, like *Faces in the Water* or *Curses in the Current* or something."

"How about *The Nymph from Nowhere*?" Caroline suggested. "How does that sound?"

"Girls!" yelled their father. "We need your help unloading before the van gets here. I've got to move the car."

Caroline took one last look over her shoulder as she followed her sisters back to the house. Picking up her own suitcase, she went upstairs, where Eddie and Beth were choosing bedrooms. She didn't much care what room she had, because as far as she was concerned, there was only one place she really belonged, and that was onstage. *Some*where in her life there was a stage, a camera, lights, and a script just for her.

"You can have this room, Caroline," Eddie said, showing her the one next to the bath.

Caroline dropped her things on the floor and went right to the window to study the river once again, Eddie leaning over her shoulder.

"Hey!" Eddie said after a moment. "Look over there!"

"Where?"

"On top of that house across the river. Do you see something moving?"

Caroline rested her chin on her hands and

squinted. She *did* see something, but she wasn't sure what.

"I'll get Dad's binoculars," she said, running downstairs and out to the car.

"Take something with you as you go," her father insisted as she started toward the house again, and Caroline picked up a bag filled with shoes.

When she returned, Beth was in her room also.

"What are you looking at?" Beth asked.

"We're not sure," said Caroline. She crouched by the window, holding the binoculars up to her eyes. Then she giggled. "*Look* at them over there! They even have field glasses!"

Beth squeezed between Caroline and Eddie and looked where her sister was pointing. "They look like leprechauns," she said.

"They're boys," Eddie told her.

"How can you tell? They could be leprechauns, chimpanzees, creatures from the black lagoon . . ."

"But what are they most *likely* to be, Beth?" Eddie insisted. "Hand her the binoculars, Caroline."

Beth took the binoculars. "Boys," she answered.

"Right."

"Spying on us!" Beth said, starting to smile.

"Right again."

"What are we going to do?"

Eddie laughed. "Give them something to look at."

"But what?"

"We'll see," said Eddie.

Caroline smiled to herself. Whatever did girls do without sisters? She took the binoculars again and watched as the four boys across the river slowly made their way back down the trapdoor in the roof.

"Whatever we do, it's got to be good," said Eddie. "If they want a show, we'll give them something to talk about."

"Like what?" Beth insisted. "Dance naked around the yard?"

Eddie gave her a pained look and was quiet a moment, thinking. At last she said, "Somebody has to die, and Caroline's it."

"Eddie!"

"Oh, just pretend," Eddie told her.

Delicious goose bumps rose up on Caroline's arms. "I hope we don't go back to Ohio," she said aloud. "I hope we *never* go back. This is so much more exciting."

"Here's what we'll do," said Eddie. "We'll wait until we see them up there spying again. Then Beth and I will go down to the river carrying Caroline."

"In a sheet," said Beth. She went to her room for a notebook and pencil and returned, scribbling as she came. "We'll be carrying Caroline in a sheet and walking real slow, crying."

"Like one of those old silent movies! Oh, Beth, that's wonderful!" Caroline said.

"When we get to the river, we'll lay her down and cry some more," Eddie continued.

"And I'll have my arms folded over my chest. I'll look like this." Caroline closed her eyes and let her lips fall open just a fraction.

"We'll have to pray over her," Beth said. "We've got to take our time."

"Okay, but when it's over, we'll tip the sheet and slide you off into the river, Caroline. You're the best one to do it because you swim like a fish," Eddie told her.

"You'll have to hold your breath and sink deep down, then swim underwater for a ways," Beth cautioned. "Make sure you climb out far up-river where there are bushes to hide you."

"And the boys will think I'm dead!" Caroline said. "Eddie, this is the most wonderful idea you've ever had. But shouldn't I have flowers?"

Flowers, Beth wrote in her notebook.

"What if Mom sees us?" Caroline wondered.

"She won't," Eddie said. "She'll be so busy moving in, she won't know where we are half the time."

Caroline, Eddie, and Beth exchanged smiles and went downstairs to help. A wonderful script and an audience, ready and waiting, Caroline thought. What more could she possibly want?

▼ ▼ ▼

It was four days later that Beth rushed in with news. She had been reading a book back in the trees near the river when she saw the boys come over the swinging bridge and sneak along the bank on the Malloys' side.

"They were dragging a large plastic bag behind them, and dumped it on our bank, right at the edge of the water." Beth panted. "And do you know what was in it? Dead fish! Dead birds! Run-over squirrels and possums! The boys want us to think the river's polluted. I heard them talking!"

"Those creepy jerks!" cried Caroline.

"Those jerky creeps!" said Eddie. "This isn't a joke anymore. This is war!"

For two more days the girls spied on the boys. Whenever they passed a window, they looked. When they went to the old garage and climbed up in the loft, they kept one eye on the house across the river. And finally, on the third morning, when Mr. and Mrs. Malloy were debating whether Mother's plants or Father's trophies should go in the sunny room on the left side of the house, Caroline looked out and saw the four boys spying on them again from the widow's walk.

She rushed into the next room and told Eddie and Beth.

"Now!" whispered Eddie.

They got a bedsheet and took it to the kitchen. Taking off her shoes, Caroline lay down on it with her arms folded across her chest. Then Beth picked up the sheet at one end, Eddie picked up the other, and they moved slowly out the back door. Step by step, with heads bent, they walked somberly down the sloping hill toward the river.

They found a spot on the bank where they were sure the boys could still see them, and then—struggling hard to keep from laughing—gently laid the bedsheet down. Caroline hoped there were no dead fish or squirrels beneath her.

"Cry," whispered Beth.

"What?" murmured Caroline, barely moving her lips.

"Not you," said Beth. "Cry, Eddie."

Eddie wasn't so good at acting, but through half-closed eyes, Caroline saw her older sister put her hands to her face, her shoulders shaking. *Wonderful.*

Beth did it much better, of course. Beth even crawled over and kissed Caroline tenderly on the forehead. It was rather nice having her sisters weep over her. Even nicer when Beth picked a few wildflowers and put them between her folded fingers. Both Beth and Eddie bowed their heads.

"Now I lay me down to sleep . . ." Eddie recited, and Beth joined in.

But then came the hard part. Caroline swallowed as she felt the sheet being lifted again. Her bottom bumped against the ground once or twice as she was carried down the bank.

Finally she felt her head begin to rise as the top

of the sheet was lifted, her feet begin to fall as the bottom of the sheet was lowered, and in what was the greatest performance of her life so far, Caroline Malloy, her body stiff as a board, eyes closed, arms still folded across her chest, slid all the way off the end of the sheet and into the chilly water.

Three

Ghost

"Did you *see* that?"

Wally crouched on the balcony beside his brothers and stared.

At first it seemed as though the two older girls were dragging a sack of garbage, and then he saw that it was the girls' youngest sister. Dead! *Obviously* dead.

Wally looked wordlessly at Jake, his mouth hanging open. *They* had only thrown a few dead fish and squirrels and possums. The new folks were throwing people!

The boys couldn't hear across the river, of course, but they had studied the small girl lying there on the sheet and she hadn't moved a finger. Not a toe. The sisters were crying like crazy, and then, like a burial at sea, they'd dumped her in the river.

"I don't believe it!" said Jake hoarsely.

"In the *river*!" said Josh.

They sat with their eyes glued to the spot in the water where the body had disappeared. The body sank way down and did not come up again, and the two sisters were walking slowly back up the hill toward the house, arms around each other, heads down.

"They must have weighted her down with stones," breathed Jake.

Wally's throat was so dry, he could hardly get the words out. "What—what do you suppose she died of?" The answer, at the back of his mind, was too awful to say aloud.

"The—the water wasn't *that* polluted," murmured Josh.

"We only took over one bag of dead stuff," said Jake.

"Anyone with a grain of sense wouldn't drink that water or swim in a river with dead animals along the bank," Josh added.

But what if she didn't know? Marty wondered. What if she hadn't seen? What if she'd gone swimming one day farther down and the germs had been carried along in the current?

"M-maybe one of those dead squirrels had a disease," he suggested finally.

"Oh, man!" Josh rested his head in his hands. "Mom's going to have a fit."

"Well, we don't *know* that the dead fish and

stuff killed her, so we aren't going to tell," Jake declared hoarsely, and looked around at the others. "Okay.? You got it? Not a word to *anybody*!"

"We can't even tell Mom the girl died?" asked Peter.

"No! Nothing! We'll wait to hear it from someone else."

Wally glanced over at Josh. He'd brought along his sketchbook because he liked to draw what houses and trees looked like from above. Josh drew things in his sketchbook that most guys never thought of drawing, but the page in front of him now was blank, and Wally was glad. He didn't want any evidence of what they had seen from the roof. If the girl had died because of what the boys had tossed on their bank, then Wally himself was a murderer because it had been his idea in the first place. He took a deep breath as he and his brothers climbed back inside.

▼ ▼ ▼

The boys were sitting soberly around the kitchen table, wondering who would find the body first, when their mother came in the back door.

"Good grief, is this how you're going to spend your last few days of vacation—just moping about?" She laid her car keys on the counter and opened the refrigerator. She had just thirty minutes to eat lunch and get back to her job at the hardware store.

"We've been busy—just taking a break," Josh told her.

"Busy doing what?" Mother asked.

Wally saw Jake give Peter a warning look. "Just messing around," Jake said.

As she passed out the sandwiches, Mother added, "I would have thought you'd be across the river by now, getting to know that new family."

"Fat chance," said Josh. "They're all girls."

"Really?" Mother looked around the table. "Somehow I had the idea there were boys."

"So did we," Jake told her.

"How many girls?" Mother asked.

"Two, now," Peter answered. "I mean three. *Three* girls!" He looked quickly at Jake. "*Three* girls, all right. I counted."

Mother studied him curiously.

"Well, at least they have children," she said, chewing thoughtfully. "It could have been worse. It could have been a family without any kids at all. I'd go over and make friends with them, if I were you."

"We will," said Jake, "when the Mississippi wears rubber pants to keep its bottom dry."

Josh laughed a little, and so did Mother, but Wally found it hard to smile at anything. Could you go to jail for planning a murder even if you didn't know anyone was going to die?

After Mother went back to work, the boys walked down to the river and followed it as far as the bridge. But they couldn't see a trace of a body— not bobbing about on the surface, not floating just beneath it, not caught in the roots of a tree or snagged on the branches that sometimes clogged the channel. The muddy water of the Buckman River moved lazily on, gracefully parting to make way for a rock here and there, then coming together again in its slow meander around the bend under the bridge.

When Father came home from work, Wally and his brothers were waiting for him on the steps. Mr. Hatford was a mailman in Buckman, and the boys knew that if anybody died anywhere at all in town, their father was one of the first to know.

"Hi, Dad," said Josh as Father came up the walk.

Mr. Hatford's shirt was damp, and he mopped his face with the small towel he carried over one shoulder in hot weather. The first thing he usually did when he got home was shower, but today he could scarcely make it into the house because the boys were blocking the steps.

"How y'doin'?" he said, maneuvering around them and going inside. The boys got up and followed him.

"Anything exciting happen today?" Jake inquired.

"I told Mrs. Blake I wouldn't deliver her mail unless she kept her dog in the house," Father said. "Almost got my pants torn off by that beast of hers. Other than that, no."

"Anybody die?" asked Peter. Wally reached over and pinched his arm, but it was too late.

"Not that I know of. Why? Did I miss something?"

"I guess we're getting bored," Jake said quickly. "Nothing exciting ever happens around here."

"Well, you could always go check out that new family," Father suggested. "Mr. Malloy is the new football coach at the college, I hear, and they've got three daughters about your ages."

"Did you meet them?" asked Josh.

"No, but I will before too long. Want me to say something for you?"

"No!" cried the four boys together.

Father smiled a little as he took off his shirt. "Okay, then. We'll just let things develop and see what happens."

What happens, Wally thought, is that someone's going to find the body, and someone is going to ask questions, and *someone*—namely Wally himself—was going to jail. All because of two words. Two words! *Dead fish.* He swallowed, but it didn't get rid of the rock in the pit of his stomach.

▾ ▾ ▾

On the last two days before school started, it seemed to Wally that he and his brothers were up on the widow's walk every waking moment, watching the new family through Mother's field glasses. He knew their name now: Malloy. Sometimes Mrs. Malloy came out to empty the trash. Sometimes Mr. Malloy drove off in his car. Once in a while Jake or Josh would catch a glimpse of the two older sisters, but the younger one was nowhere in sight.

"Do you suppose she's *not* dead?" Wally asked hopefully. "Maybe they only thought she was dead, but the water revived her and she swam back to the bank."

"So why haven't we seen her around?" asked Jake. "Why do we see the two older sisters but we never see her?"

"She's sick, maybe?" suggested Peter.

"No, she's dead, all right," said Josh. He had drawn a picture of what the youngest Malloy girl would look like after being dead in the river for several days. Wally wished he hadn't drawn it, but Peter studied the picture with wide eyes.

If the Bensons were still here, Wally thought, they would have helped look for the body. *They* would have had some good ideas about where it could be. Then he remembered that if the Bensons were here, the Malloys would not be. What *would* he be doing if the Bensons were back?

Well, he decided, he and Bill Benson would probably have figured out by now what made the rows of little holes in the trunk of the pear tree. Sapsuckers, he had thought, but his friend had said bees. They had even been going to camp out all night and take turns watching, just to find out. Now they never would. Now there were girls to watch instead.

Wally spent most of his time lying in the grass behind the house, staring up at the sky. Peter lay down beside him.

"Do you see that spiderweb, Wally?" Peter asked, pointing to the thin strands of silver spun between a forsythia bush and a lilac. "Do you suppose the spider spins the cross ones first or the down ones?"

Wally often wondered that himself. "I think," he said, looking hard at the web, "that the spider sort of goes across and down at the same time—just drifts down hanging by a thread. Pretty clever, when you—"

"And if the thread breaks, splat!" said Peter delightedly, whapping one hand on the ground.

Wally sighed.

▼ ▼ ▼

Usually there was at least *some* excitement connected with going back to school in the fall. This year Mother had bought them all new T-shirts and jeans, and Wally and Peter had picked out new sneakers as well. But the boys hadn't put paper in their notebooks yet. They hadn't even sharpened their pencils. The big question among the boys was what they would say to the girls when the two remaining Malloy sisters walked across the bridge the next day on their way to school.

Mother didn't come home for lunch, so Jake

made beans and franks. "Why don't we watch from an upstairs window tomorrow, and when we see them start across the bridge, we'll time it so we get out to the road when they do. I just want to hear what they have to say about their sister," he said.

"What if they don't say anything?" Wally asked. "We don't even know their names. We can't just say, 'Hey, so-and-so, how's what's-her-name?' "

"We could say, 'How is the sister we saw rolled up in a bedsheet?' " Peter suggested. Josh shot him a disgusted glance, and Peter went back to lining the beans up in rows on his plate, then stabbing them three at a time with his fork.

The following morning Jake and Josh crouched at an upstairs window, watching the bridge. Peter, with his new lunch box, waited below.

Wally, however, was still dressing. As he put on his new sneakers, he realized that the treads were so deep, he could probably roll up a tiny piece of paper and stick it in a groove without it falling out. If he ever had to carry a secret somewhere, and there was any danger of being searched, he could always wear a new pair of sneakers and—

"They're coming!" Josh yelled.

Like a whirlwind the twins rushed downstairs, where Peter was waiting. With Wally bringing up the rear they all went outside.

The two older Malloy sisters, wearing jeans and long shirts down to their knees, were walking arm in arm across the swinging bridge, leaning on each other, heads together, like two girls who had more sadness than they could possibly bear, Wally thought.

As they came closer, the Hatford brothers pretended to be looking down the road, at the sky, anywhere, in fact, except at the Malloys.

"Ask!" Jake whispered to Josh.

"*You* ask!" said Josh. "You always try to make me do it."

"Wally, you do it," said Jake.

"Why me? What the heck am I supposed to say?"

The girls had reached the middle of the narrow bridge now and, still walking side by side, held on to the cable handrails as the bridge bounced slightly beneath their weight.

"If one of us doesn't ask, Peter will," Josh warned. "He'll say something dumb, like 'Have you buried anyone lately?' "

"I will not!" snapped Peter.

Wally didn't know what he'd say, but he knew that someone had to say something, so he stepped out in front of his brothers and started toward the bridge.

But suddenly there was nothing at all to say, because, as he stared, the two older Malloy girls stepped off the end of the bridge and the third Malloy sister popped out from behind them. She came right down the path to the very spot where Wally was standing. She had either never been dead at all or she was the first ghost in the history of Buckman, and here she was now, in front of his very eyes.

Four

Conversation

"This," said Caroline to her sisters as the Hatford boys headed up the sidewalk, "was our greatest performance yet."

"What do you mean *yet*?" asked Beth, pulling a paperback from her bookbag to finish before school. *The Fog People,* it said on the cover. "I'm not going to spend all my time dropping you in the river and hiding you on the bridge."

"But they believed! They really, truly believed that I was dead and buried at sea! The look on their faces when I came out from behind you! If we could carry that off, we could do anything. We'd make a wonderful team!"

The four Hatford brothers were growing smaller and smaller in the distance. They hadn't said hello or 'Welcome to Buckman' or anything at all. They'd just gaped, their mouths wide open.

Eddie whirled her baseball cap around on one finger. "You *know* they'll try to get even."

"We *are* even! They dumped dead fish and squirrels on our side of the river, and we spooked them into thinking I was dead," said Caroline. She almost wished they *weren't* even, because she had so many wonderful scenes yet to play. There must be a hundred and fifty ways she and Beth and Eddie could fool the boys. Boys made such a wonderful audience. They'd believe anything.

Buckman Elementary was an old building of dark redbrick that didn't look anything like the new school they had left behind in Ohio.

"Quaint," said Beth, when she saw it.

"Dismal," Eddie proclaimed.

Caroline hadn't decided what to think about it until she passed the auditorium with its high stage and velvet curtain.

She stopped in her tracks and stared. Back in Ohio the only auditorium was the cafeteria. There the stage was a foot off the floor, with no curtain at all. But here there were fixed rows of seats for the audience, the kind you saw in movie theaters, and the curtain was maroon on one side, gold on the other. She knew positively when she saw it that somehow, sometime, on that very stage, she and Beth and Eddie would perform, and that she, Caroline Lenore Malloy, would have the leading role.

What she did *not* expect was that she would find

herself in the same classroom with one of the boys across the river. She didn't even know his name, but she recognized him from his sneakers that morning.

"Welcome to fourth grade," said a large woman at the front of the room—a woman as round and rosy as an apple, whose name was—incredible as it looked there on the blackboard—Miss Applebaum.

If Caroline weren't so precocious, she would have been entering the third grade, because she was only eight. But she had learned to read at four, subtract by five, and when she was six, she was in first grade only a month before she was transferred to second. If she was surprised to find herself in the same room with one of the boys across the river, however, the boy himself seemed even more astonished. His eyes grew as large as turnips when Caroline came through the door and his face turned petunia-pink.

"If you can remember just one thing, class, we'll get along famously," Miss Applebaum was saying. "When I talk, you listen. Now, the first thing we're going to do is seat you alphabetically."

I sure hope his last name isn't Mahony or something, Caroline thought, watching the boy.

Miss Applebaum was calling out names of students and pointing to seats, one after another, in the first row. She called out, "Wally Hatford," and pointed to the first seat in the second row, and the boy took it.

Wally Hatford, huh? Caroline said to herself.

Well, the Hatfords would soon find out they were no match for the Malloys. Miss Applebaum was filling up the rest of the second row, and when she called out, "Caroline Malloy," Caroline realized that the apple-shaped teacher was pointing to a desk directly behind Wally.

Caroline quietly took her seat, and hardly dared move. She was sure that the moment the teacher's back was turned, the boy would turn around and say something so awful, so embarrassing about Caroline and her sisters tricking him and his brothers that she would be forced to think of something awful and embarrassing to do to him next.

Wally did not turn around, however. He said nothing at all, and Caroline could not stand it. He kept his head pointing straight forward, hands on his desk, where he was holding a ruler between his thumbs, and as Miss Applebaum droned on and on, Caroline leaned forward and blew, ever so gently, at the fine hairs on the back of his neck.

This time she saw goose bumps break out on Wally's skin. Caroline smiled to herself. She leaned forward even farther until her mouth was just inches away from Wally's left ear, and then she said, "Wal-ly."

The boy did not move, but his ear—*both* ears—turned bright red.

"Wal-ly," Caroline whispered again, just behind him. "There is a gigantic black spider with eight hairy legs dropping down from the ceiling about five inches above your head."

"Where?" Wally said, throwing back his head, and crashed right into Caroline's nose.

"Ow!" she yelped, covering her face.

"Caroline Malloy and Wally Hatford!" said Miss Applebaum. "I don't believe either of you is paying the slightest attention. What's wrong?"

"There was a big spider coming down from the ceiling over my head," said Wally. "She told me."

He seemed to be trying hard not to smile, but Caroline could hardly think because her nose ached so.

Miss Applebaum came down the aisle and stood beside her. "Let's see this gigantic spider," she said dryly. "A spider like that we should study in science. Where is it?"

"Gone, I guess," Caroline said, still holding her nose. It was bleeding a little. She hoped it wasn't broken. Actresses with broken noses never got the good parts.

"Since Caroline and Wally have cost us some class time, I think it would be fair for them to stay after school and make it up," said Miss Applebaum. "If you see any more big hairy spiders, Caroline, you may collect them in a paste jar. And if you hear any other girls telling you about spiders descending over your head, Wally, I suggest you pay no attention whatever. Do you want to see the nurse, Caroline?"

"No." Caroline answered, snuffling, and spent the rest of class with a tissue wadded beneath her nose.

She didn't see her sisters all morning. When the fourth grade was doing arithmetic, the fifth and sixth grades were having recess. When the fourth grade was having recess, the fifth and sixth grades were having lunch.

It was halfway through the afternoon when Caroline happened to pass Eddie's class in the hall on the way to the library. She grabbed her sister's arm and said, "Eddie, is my nose broken?"

"What?"

"Is it crooked?"

"No. What happened?"

"Wally Hatford."

"What?" cried Eddie, but by this time her classmates were well down the hall, and she had to run to catch up.

What bothered Caroline most about her predicament was that she wouldn't be able to walk home with Beth and Eddie, and would have to wait to tell them about Wally Hatford banging her nose.

At three o'clock everyone left except Caroline and Wally.

"What is so wrong about not listening when I'm talking," Miss Applebaum told them, "is that you disturb other students as well."

Caroline stared down at her desktop. She wondered how old it was. There were all kinds of things scratched in the wood—initials and numbers and little cartoon faces.

"And because listening is the most important thing in my class, and talking out of turn is so distracting," Miss Applebaum continued, "I want to make sure it doesn't happen again. Come up here, both of you."

Caroline got woodenly to her feet. Miss Applebaum wasn't going to paddle them, was she? She didn't think she could stand the humiliation. Wasn't that against the law? Or could teachers do things like that in West Virginia?

She followed Wally up front where Miss Applebaum was placing two chairs, face to face, about three feet apart.

"I want you to sit here," she told them, "and I want you to talk to each other for ten minutes. Perhaps at the end of that time you will have said everything there is to say, and there will be no more disturbances in class."

No! Caroline thought. She would rather be paddled! One minute would be bad enough, five minutes would be cruel and unusual punishment, and ten was torture!

She lowered herself sideways into one of the chairs. What was she supposed to say to a boy who, up until that morning, had thought she was dead?

Miss Applebaum stood with arms folded. "Well? I'm waiting."

Caroline crossed her ankles. "You started it," she said to Wally.

"What did *I* do?" he mumbled, sitting sideways himself.

"Dumping all that dead stuff on our side of the river."

"So *you* pretended to die."

"Is this a normal conversation?" asked Miss Applebaum as she picked up a box of supplies and headed for the closet at the back of the room.

"No," said Caroline, but she was talking to Wally, not her teacher. "This is not a normal conversation because you and your brothers aren't normal human beings. Normal people don't go dumping dead fish and birds around the neighborhood."

"It wasn't my idea," said Wally. "Well, actually it *was* my idea—dead fish, I mean—but it was Jake and Josh who—"

"So *none* of you are normal."

"*We're* not normal?" said Wally, his voice rising. "What do you call people who go burying each other in the river?"

"It was a great performance, and you know it."

"It was dumb."

"You believed I was dead."

"I believe you're crazy."

"We'll see about that."

"Whatever you two are arguing about, you'd better get it out of your systems now, because when you come to school tomorrow, I expect you to pay attention," Miss Applebaum called, sticking her head out of the supply closet.

"You and your dumb brothers," Caroline muttered because she couldn't think of anything else to say.

"You and your stupid sisters," said Wally.

"We're smarter than the four of you put together," Caroline told him.

"We'll see," said Wally.

"If you'd just left us alone instead of dumping that dead stuff, things would be okay," said Caroline.

"If you'd go back where you came from, there wouldn't be any more trouble," Wally replied.

"Oh, yeah? If you went back to where *you* came from, you'd be in a cave!"

"That does it," said Wally, hotly. "The war is on."

"Okay," called Miss Applebaum, coming back to the front of the room for another box. "If you two have settled things, you may leave now." She looked from Caroline to Wally. "Unless, of course, you are not agreed."

"We agree," said Caroline emphatically. *The war is definitely on.*

She could hardly wait to get home and tell her sisters.

What she discovered when she got outside was that she wasn't the only member of her family who had been kept after school. Eddie had stumbled over Jake's foot in the cafeteria and, sure that he'd tripped her on purpose, brought her tray down on his head. Beth, of course, had waited for Eddie, so there they were again, the three of them coming home late on the very first day.

Mother was dusting shelves in the hallway. "Whatever happened to your nose?" she asked, looking at Caroline.

"She bumped into something that needs a little fixing," said Beth.

"Needs a lot of straightening out," put in Eddie.

"Well, how was school?" Mother asked.

"Urk," said Eddie.

"Ugh," said Beth.

"It has possibilities," said Caroline.

Five

Peace Offering

Peter, Josh, and Jake were waiting in the bushes when Wally came around the bend.

"What happened?" asked Jake. "The Malloys just stomped by, mad as anything."

Wally was miserable. "I just declared war," he said, and told them what had happened.

"Hoo boy!" Josh whistled.

"Wow!" said Peter.

For the rest of the way home Jake and Josh talked about what they would do if the Malloys tried to get even with Wally for bumping Caroline's nose. They were in the same class with Eddie.

"That Eddie would try anything," said Jake. "If she'd dump her tray on me in front of teachers and everybody, you can imagine what she'd do when no one was looking."

"Did you watch her pitch at recess? Whomp!

The ball comes at you before you can look at it cross-eyed," Josh went on.

"Who's the other sister?" Peter asked, walking fast to keep up.

"Beth," Josh told him. "She's weird. Sits on the steps at recess and reads a book."

"A Whomper, a Weirdo, and a Crazie," said Jake, and sighed. "I wonder how the Benson guys are doing down in Georgia. I'll bet they miss us like anything."

When they reached the house, Wally took a box of crackers up to his room and sat on the floor to eat them, his back against his bed. He still couldn't believe that he was the one who had officially declared war on the Malloys. How had it happened? Only a week before he was lying on his back in the grass, and now here he was: Number One on their Most-Wanted list. He was on bad terms already with his teacher, had almost broken Caroline's nose, and had made everything worse by calling her sisters stupid.

Well, they *were* stupid. And deep down, seven layers beneath his skin, Wally knew he was glad that he had thrust his head back and bumped Caroline. He'd just wanted her to stop bugging him, that's all. But her nose sure looked peculiar by the end of the day—a lot redder and fatter than it had looked that morning.

Then he had another thought: What if it really was broken, she had to have an operation, and he had to pay for it? His hands began to sweat, and he swallowed the piece of cracker in his mouth without chewing. Was there such a thing as just a sprained nose? A bruised nose? A slightly but not completely fractured nose? A bent nose, maybe?

Peter came into Wally's room and sat down beside him on the rug.

"What are we going to do next?" he asked excitedly, helping himself to a cracker. He rested one hand on Wally's leg, looking up at his older brother.

What Wally wanted to do, in fact, was sit on this rug for the rest of his natural life and never have to face the Malloys again.

"You're the general," said Peter.

"Huh?"

"That's what Josh said. He said you're the one who declared the war, so you've got to call the shots. That's what he said, all right."

Wally gave a low moan.

"What I think we should do," said Peter, "is dig a large hole and cover it with leaves and sticks, and when Caroline and her sisters walk across it, they'll fall in and we'll keep them trapped forever."

"Go out and play, Peter," Wally told him.

▼ ▼ ▼

The boys were strangely quiet when their father came home from his mail route about four. Jake was planning strategies in a notebook, Josh was drawing a picture of Eddie dropping her tray on Jake, just for the record, and Peter was building a pit out of toothpicks, then running a Matchbox car over it and watching the car tumble in. Wally was looking out the window, wondering how far away he could get if he climbed on the first Greyhound through town.

Mr. Hatford took off his cap and went out to the kitchen for a Mountain Dew. Then he leaned against the doorway and looked at the boys. "You'll be interested to know that the Malloy girls are Eddie, Beth, and Caroline."

"*Tell* me about it," Jake mumbled.

"The way their mother described them, they sound like three live wires to me."

"Crossed wires is more like it," said Josh.

"Short circuits," said Wally.

"A Whomper, a Weirdo, and a Crazie," Peter repeated.

Mr. Hatford frowned. "You boys can either make yourselves miserable by wishing the Bensons were back, which they're not, or you can enjoy a great September day, which it is. And I, for one, aim to enjoy the day." He took his soft drink out onto the side porch along with the paper.

Jake looked at Josh. "I'll bet they'll spread it all over town how they tricked us. Everyone will be laughing."

"You know what we could do, don't you?" said Josh. "Totally ignore them. Freeze them out. Not even give them the time of day."

"If we see them coming, we could just turn and walk the other way," said Peter.

"We can't," said Jake. "Wally declared war."

"Oh, yeah. Right," said Josh.

Hoo boy! thought Wally.

▾ ▾ ▾

The hardware store was open till nine most evenings, and this was Mrs. Hatford's night to work. When she popped in about six to make dinner, she said, "Boys, I've got a job for you. I baked a cake this morning before work, frosted it at noon, and I want you to take it over to the Malloys right now so they can have some with their supper."

Wally stared at his mother as though she had just grown another head.

"Well, don't look so astonished," she said, coming out of the kitchen with a large square box. "It's the traditional way to greet a new family in the neighborhood, you know. The Bensons did it for us the first week we moved in, and I'll never forget how good that cake tasted after unpacking all day."

"But—" Wally began.

"Just hand it to whoever answers the door, tell them it's from the Hatfords, and say, 'Welcome to Buckman.' That's all you have to say. Then come right home because dinner's almost ready."

"Could we—could we just leave it on their porch?" Wally asked.

"Wallace Hatford, you certainly may not!" his mother scolded. "A dog could get into it, there might be a rain . . . all sorts of things could happen. What's the matter with saying a few cordial words to a new family? Hurry up, now. Who's going to take it over?"

Wally looked at Jake, who was looking at Josh, and then they all turned toward Peter.

"Peter is not going over there alone. This is a three-layer chocolate chiffon with whipped cream frosting, and I worked on it a total of two hours and set it on the plate I got from Aunt Ida at Christmas. I want to make sure it gets there in one piece. You can *all* go. Hold this box steady, now," she instructed, thrusting it into Wally's hands. "If the cake slides around, the icing will come off on the sides of the box. Tell them there's no hurry about returning the plate."

Wally and his brothers moved down the front steps as though they were headed for a funeral and Wally carried the remains of the deceased in the box. *This can't be happening,* he said to himself, but it was. After half breaking Caroline's nose, this would look as though he were saying he was sorry. He was *not* sorry, and now he was mad as anything.

"If Caroline comes to the door, Wally, let her have it," said Jake. "Swoosh! Right in the schnozz. It'll be worth the whipping we get when we go home."

"Uh-uh," said Josh. "Dad'll march us back over there and make us apologize, and that would be worse."

"*You* take it," Wally said, holding the box out toward Jake. "Eddie dropped her tray on you in the cafeteria, and you could drop this on her. We'd just say we were getting even."

"No way. I'd still have to apologize, and I'm not about to apologize to Eddie Malloy if someone burned my feet with hot irons."

"Wow!" said Peter, impressed.

They walked down the sidewalk, crossed the road, and started along the bank toward the swinging footbridge.

"I know what we can do," Wally said at last. "We could creep over to their front porch, set the cake in front of the door, then ring the bell and run. That way we wouldn't have to say anything at all."

"*If* we can get over there without their seeing us," said Josh.

"Here's what we'll do," Jake told them. "Once we get across the bridge, we'll stay off Island Avenue and keep to the bushes along the river. When we get opposite their house, we'll put the cake on the porch when no one's watching."

"This isn't any fun," grumbled Peter. "I thought this was a war."

"Just a temporary cease-fire," Jake assured him.

The boys had just stepped onto the swinging bridge and started across when Wally's heart almost stopped beating, for coming down the hill on the other side were the three Malloy sisters, and a moment later they, too, were on the bridge.

For a moment everybody stopped, the Hatfords at one end, the Malloys at the other.

"Now what?" whispered Wally.

"They're trying to block us," said Jake. "Just keep going. If they want a fight, they'll get it."

The boys started forward again. The girls moved forward too.

The swinging bridge bounced and jiggled as the two groups came toward each other. Wally held on to the cable with one hand, the cake with the other. He'd never fought a girl in his life. None of his brothers had, either, and he knew that for all of Jake's talk, they wouldn't begin now. This was a different kind of battle—a war of the wits.

But what if the girls didn't see it that way? What if the Malloys got out in the middle of the bridge and trashed them? Could they fight back then?

The Hatford brothers had fallen into single file as they approached the middle of the bridge. You always did that when you met someone coming toward you; always said hello and moved over to make room. The Malloy girls, however, came in a row.

"The first one who tries anything gets the cake right in the puss," Jake whispered in Wally's ear.

The next thing Wally knew, he was face to face with Caroline Malloy—face to nose, anyway, for her swollen nose seemed to take up half her face. It had also turned black and blue. He realized suddenly that if he just gave the girls the cake, he wouldn't have to walk all the way over to their house. He wouldn't have to ring the doorbell and say nice things to the parents. He wouldn't have to fight the girls to get on across either.

"Here," he said, holding the box out in front of him. "It's a cake."

Caroline stared at him, then at her sisters.

"It's a *cake*!" Wally said again. "It's for you."

"Yeah?" said Eddie.

"I'll just bet!" said Beth. "What dead animal did you dream up this time?"

Suddenly Caroline grabbed the box out of Wally's hands and, in one swift toss, flung it over the side of the bridge.

Wally and his brothers stared in astonishment as Mother's three-layer chocolate chiffon spilled out into the water, the two top layers heading in different directions. The box—with the bottom layer still in it—bobbed up and down in the current, and the whipped cream frosting, like foam, floated downstream.

Six

The River on Caroline

Caroline and her sisters stood with their hands over their mouths, eyes like fried eggs.

"Oh, Lordy!" gasped Caroline. "It really *was* a cake!"

The box below was sailing away.

"Enjoy!" said Wally, grinning. "Don't forget to return the plate."

With that the four Hatford brothers turned around and went back toward their side of the river, though the youngest lingered just long enough for one last look in the water. "Wow!" he said.

"What are we going to *do*?" Caroline cried to her sisters.

"Don't ask *me*!" said Beth. "You're the one who threw it in."

"But you didn't believe it was a cake, either, Beth. You know you didn't!"

"We're in this together," Eddie agreed. "*I* probably would have taken the box and dumped it over their heads."

"I suppose we could always say we ate it," Caroline mused, watching the whipped cream frosting leave a long trail in its wake. And then she cried suddenly, "The plate! We've got to return the plate!"

The box seemed to be floating toward the Malloys' side of the river. The girls ran back across the bridge and down the bank to the water's edge.

"There it is!" Eddie shouted. She looked at Caroline. "Go for it."

"It's not fair!" Caroline cried. "We're in this together, you said."

"Okay, we *all* go in," decided Eddie, and the girls took off their shoes and socks, and rolled up their jeans.

The water did not seem as warm as it had been a week ago when Caroline slid off the sheet and disappeared into the muddy brown of the Buckman River. Now it was almost six in the evening, August had become September, and that little change made a difference.

The riverbed was rocky in places, and where it was bare, thick mud oozed up between Caroline's toes. Now and then something tickled her ankles as she waded out toward the center, and she did not even like to think what it might be.

The box had stopped at a pile of brush in the river, but one corner appeared to be sinking.

"Hurry, Caroline!" Beth yelled, plodding along behind.

Caroline took a deep breath and waded in up to her waist. The more water-logged her jeans became, the heavier they felt, and the harder it was to walk.

"Hurry!" Beth screeched again.

Caroline took a giant step forward this time, but her foot slipped on the slimy bottom. The last thing she saw before the water washed over her was the white box rising up over the debris with the current, and sailing on downstream.

Glub, glub, glub. Water filled her ears, her nose —clouded her eyes. Gasping, she reared up, all her clothes heavy now. Before she could see anything, however, she could hear shrieks of laughter from the opposite bank, and knew that the Hatford boys had been watching.

"We'll get *them*!" Eddie called. "Don't pay any attention, Caroline. Just get the plate."

But the box was moving faster than the girls could keep up, and—what's more—seemed to be sinking slowly at the same time. More hoots from the boys. Caroline began to swim.

Caroline Lenore, she told herself, *you are an actress, and actresses don't pay any attention to distractions. Make this your greatest performance yet.*

And so, as she swam toward the center of the Buckman River where she had last seen the box, she pretended that she was a young mother swimming, swimming, desperately swimming, to rescue her small child before he disappeared forever beneath the waves.

Caroline tried to concentrate on her face. She would have a look of agonized terror, she decided, opening her eyes wide, teeth frozen behind half-parted lips, little gasps coming from her throat. She could see the Hatford boys back on the far bank, watching.

The camera would move in for a close-up of her face, and just then she would close her eyes, and . . . plunge. Caroline went tail up like a duck, diving beneath the surface, her arms outstretched, feeling for a box or a china plate. Once she thought she touched it, but it was only the slimy moss of a rock.

"There it goes!" shouted Beth, pointing farther downstream as Caroline surfaced. "Oh, m'gosh, it's headed for the rocks!"

Her baby! Her poor baby! The cameras still rolling in her head, Caroline plunged forward again, arms battling the water as she stroked. Faster, faster . . . her only child! In another minute he would be dashed against the rocks.

Out of the corner of her eye she could see the Hatford boys going home. They weren't even going to stay till the end! No matter. A good actress played her part whether or not the entire theater was empty. On she swam.

The box came apart just before the largest rock in the river came into view. She could see the plate spilling out, sinking, and she lunged. She had it!

She'd found him! She'd rescued her little baby, her heart's delight!

Holding the plate against her chest, Caroline crawled up on the rock and swooned.

"For corn's sake, Caroline, cut the comedy!" Eddie yelled, swimming toward her. She and Beth reached the rock and climbed up beside Caroline, who collapsed dramatically against them, going limp in their arms.

"Caroline, knock it off!" Eddie said sternly. "Is the plate okay?"

The mood was broken; the show was over. Caroline blinked, her hair streaming water into her eyes, and examined the plate. It still had a sticker on the bottom, as though it were new, and there was a dainty scalloped design around the edge—the kind of plate her mother used for cookies at Christmas, or served little sandwiches on when she entertained the faculty wives. Miraculously it was not broken, but there was a fine hairline crack in the surface. "It's okay, I guess," she told Eddie.

Eddie and Beth slipped into the water again, and Caroline reluctantly followed, swimming back to the bank behind her sisters.

"What are we going to tell Mom?" Beth asked as they put on their socks and sneakers. "What will we say about the cake?"

"Never mind the cake, what will we tell her about *us*?" said Eddie. "Look at us! Soaked to the skin!"

▼ ▼ ▼

Dinner at the Malloys was almost never before seven, because Coach Malloy had football practice until six-thirty every evening in the fall. The girls had just time enough to rush upstairs to shower and change before they saw his car making its way down Island Avenue, to park at last in the clearing between the house and garage.

He slid into his chair at the table. "You girls look as though you'd been swimming" was the first thing out of his mouth.

"In *that* river?" asked Mother, placing a roast before them.

"I just took a shower," said Beth, which was the honest truth.

"Me too," said Eddie.

"Well, that's where I'm headed after dinner," their father said. "I don't know if I've got a team or not, Jean, they all seem pretty green to me. But I'll tell you one thing, I'm going to make them one by the first of October."

"Of course you will," said Mrs. Malloy. "You know, I sort of like living in a small town like this."

"*I* think it stinks," said Eddie, reaching for the pepper.

Her mother looked up. "Why, Edith Ann?"

"It's a town full of dumb boys, is what it is, and I pitched better than any boy at recess today, but I *still* have to try out for the baseball team."

"It's only fair," said her father. "Have you met any of the neighbors?"

"I have," said Mrs. Malloy. "The people next door are friendly. And I met our mailman for the first time, a Mr. Hatford. He says he lives across the river, and his wife works at Grady's Hardware. By and by, I imagine, we'll meet them all."

Caroline looked at Beth and Eddie and said nothing. But after dinner, when Mother went upstairs to write some letters and the girls were on kitchen duty, she said, "You know what we have to do, don't you? Return the plate."

"You know what will happen if the boys answer the door; they'll take the plate, break it, and tell their mother we did it," Beth said.

"Then we've got to make sure the mother's there when we ring the doorbell. In fact, we'll ask to talk to her," said Caroline.

Eddie went to the telephone in the hall and looked up the number for Grady's Hardware, then dialed. "What time do you close?" she asked.

"Nine o'clock," a man told her.

Eddie hung up and looked at the others. "We leave here at nine-fifteen, and we'd better figure out exactly what we're going to say."

"Right!" said Caroline. "Beth, you write the script, and we'll practice it a couple times first."

▼ ▼ ▼

At a quarter past nine the girls crossed the bridge in the moonlight, the plate securely in Eddie's hands. It was a beautiful night, almost too lovely to be angry at anyone, Caroline thought. Beth must have felt the same way because, halfway over, she said, "Why do you suppose the Hatford boys hate us so much?"

"I don't think they *hate* us," Caroline mused. "I'll bet they're just mad that the Bensons moved out and we moved in. The Bensons had all boys, you know."

"Well, too bad!" Eddie snapped. "I didn't ask to come here any more than they wanted me to."

"I suppose we *could* just ring the doorbell and say, 'Look, let's bury the hatchet and be friends,' " Beth suggested.

The girls looked at each other and smiled a little.

"Naw," said Caroline. "This is a lot more fun."

The porch light was still on when the Malloy girls went up the steps to the Hatfords' large porch, which wrapped around three sides of the house. Through the curtains they could see Mr. Hatford stretched out on the couch, watching TV, and a boy somewhere in the background, who seemed to be doing his homework at the dining-room table.

Caroline pressed the button. The doorbell chimed. Footsteps. The door opened. And there was Wally Hatford, his eyes wide.

"Who is it, Wally?" came a woman's voice in the background.

"It—it's . . ."

"Who?"

A woman appeared and Wally disappeared—disappeared as though the floor had opened and swallowed him up.

"Hello, Mrs. Hatford," Caroline said sweetly. "We came to return your cake plate."

"My goodness, so soon? There was no hurry."

"It was wonderful," said Beth. "Chocolate is my favorite. Chocolate cake with whipped cream frosting."

"Well, it was an old recipe, but it always works well for me. Chocolate chiffon, it was, to be exact." Mrs. Hatford looked pleased.

"Right. Chocolate chiffon," said Eddie. "Thanks a lot."

"We want our neighbors to feel welcome," Mrs. Hatford told her. "If there is anything at all we can do to help you get settled, we'd be glad to. The boys, also."

An actress, Caroline knew, had to be ready to ad-lib when the occasion arose, and that occasion was now.

"Oh, I know there would be lots of things Dad could use boys for, seeing as how he has only girls," Caroline said.

"Well, you just let us know—any chores at all," said Mrs. Hatford. "Call us anytime, and I'll send them right over."

Seven

Free-for-all

Wally stood motionless in the hallway as his mother closed the door.

"Well, they certainly must have enjoyed that cake, to eat it all in one meal," she said. She turned the plate over in her hands, then frowned. "My goodness, it's cracked! You'd think they would have taken better care of it, wouldn't you?"

Wally started to tell her what had happened to the plate, but stopped. If he said any more, he'd have to explain why the girls had thrown it in the river. And if he told why, he'd have to tell about the dead fish and the way he'd banged Caroline's nose in class.

"They probably fed it to a dog," he said lamely.

Mother wheeled about. "Wallace, I don't know what's got into you lately. *All* you boys have been on edge. Maybe you don't have enough to do. Need a few extra chores around here."

Hoo boy! thought Wally as he went upstairs.

This evening sure hadn't turned out the way he'd wanted. He and his brothers had had a laughing fit watching Caroline out there in the river, trying to find that plate. He never thought she would, and the boys would have waited around if they hadn't remembered that dinner was on the table.

Wally lay on his stomach on his bed and stared down at the braided rug. Ordinarily he would have tried to figure out just how the little loops of orange got hooked onto the loops of green—where it all began, and which piece you'd have to pull first if you wanted the whole thing to come unraveled, but now he was too mad at the Malloys to give it much thought.

He'd like to pull a loop on the Malloy sisters, that's what, and watch them come apart for once. He'd like to see them pack their bags and take off out of town at seventy miles an hour.

It just wasn't like it was when the Bensons lived in Buckman. Back then they always signed each other's notebooks on the first day of school—the Hatfords and the Bensons. They'd give each other new nicknames for the year, and once they'd all taken the names of football players. That was the year Wally had been Joe Montana. Things were sure different now. Caroline and her black-and-blue nose! Eddie and that dumb cap! Beth and those stupid books she read.

She'd left one on the steps a few minutes at recess, Josh had reported, and he'd seen the cover: *Fang, King of the Vampires.* What kind of a girl would read a book like that? Weirdo was right.

▼ ▼ ▼

When the Hatford boys were ready for school the next day, they watched until the Malloys were across the bridge and well up the sidewalk before they set out themselves.

"You see what's happening, don't you?" Jake grumbled. "They're running our lives! They've only been here a week, and already we can't even leave for school when we want; we make sure they've got there first."

"And Mom thinks they're nice! They're poison!" said Josh.

Wally did not turn around in his seat once to look at Caroline, and she didn't bother him—no blowing on the back of his neck or whispering in his ear. At lunchtime he sat as far away from her table as he could get, and when he left at the end of the day, Miss Applebaum said, "Thank you, Wally, for being a good listener." He could have puked.

Jake and Josh and Peter were waiting for him when he came out. Josh had a smile on his face.

"What have *you* got to grin about?" Wally asked.

"At recess this afternoon," Josh told him, "I went inside for a drink of water, and when I came out again, there's Beth, on the bottom step, reading her stupid book."

"Fang, King of the Vampires?" Wally asked.

Josh nodded and grinned even wider. "I had my jacket tied around my shoulders, and when I spread out my arms, I looked like a giant bat. All I did was come slowly down the steps behind her, and she screamed her head off. I didn't even touch her."

Jake and Wally and Peter all laughed.

"You get caught?" asked Wally.

"No, but boy, was she mad! She said this was exactly the kind of thing that gives her nightmares, and I said, well, why did she read books like that if they gave her nightmares? Stupid thing!"

"Ha!" said Jake.

Home again, Wally had just poured himself a glass of Hi-C, and the boys were making peanut-butter-and-cracker sandwiches, when the phone rang. Wally answered.

"Listen," came his mother's voice, and she was beginning to sound like Miss Applebaum. "Your father was talking with Mrs. Malloy this morning on his route, and she wondered who she could hire to wash their windows. Dad told her you boys have more time on your hands than is good for you, and that you'd come over after school and help. Now, I don't want you to expect payment."

Wally yelped.

"Wally?" said his mother.

"It's not fair!" he shouted. "They've got three girls who could wash windows. Eddie can climb up a ladder as well as any of us, and she's even taller than Josh. Besides, I've got plenty of things to do!"

"Name one," said his mother.

Wally stood speechless. He didn't have any homework to do; he didn't play on any team. He didn't even need a haircut. He did, of course, still want to see how long it took a waffle box to go around the river, but . . .

"Wallace Hatford, you and your brothers have yourselves a snack and get on over to the Malloys'. With the four of you working, you could have their windows done in no time, and it's the least we can do for new neighbors. Why, when we moved in, the Bensons came over and helped us wallpaper the dining room. I'll never forget it. And I don't want to hear any arguments."

The receiver clicked, and Wally stood staring at the phone in his hand. He didn't have to tell the others; they'd already heard.

"We've got to wash their windows, right?" said Josh.

"Right," said Wally. "I'll bet Caroline put her mother up to this! Went right home and told her how much we wanted to help! And Dad probably said we'd do it for nothing."

"I'll wash their windows, all right," muttered Jake. "I'll put out their lights, curl their hair, and knock them into the middle of next week."

"Gosh!" said Peter.

"They're getting too cocky!" Jake went on.

"Those girls think they can get away with anything. They need a good scare, that's what. Then maybe they'll leave us alone."

"But how?" asked Peter.

Everyone turned to Wally.

"I'll think of something," Wally told them.

▼ ▼ ▼

By the time they finished their snack and headed off toward the Malloys', the boys had given up any idea of trying to scare the entire family. But they *were* convinced that they could scare Beth half out of her mind, and the thought of it, the vision of it, the sweet taste of victory in their mouths, made the idea of washing all the Malloys' windows worth it, every window.

It would have been better, of course, if Caroline, Beth, and Eddie were not smirking at them as they came across the lawn. Were not, in fact, sitting on a blanket out on the grass, sunning themselves, with cookies and soft drinks beside them, ready to enjoy the show.

"I'm so glad to meet you," said Mrs. Malloy, coming down the steps. "Your dad said you were the best window washers around, and I think it's wonderful the way you offered to help."

Wally didn't know whether he imagined it or whether he really did hear a snicker from Caroline.

"You do know each other, don't you?" Mrs. Malloy went on, motioning to the girls on the lawn.

"Eddie, Beth, and Caroline, this is . . ." She paused, waiting for the boys to say their own names.

"Josh," said Jake.

"Jake," said Josh.

"Peter," said Wally.

"Wally," said Peter.

Wally could hardly keep from grinning. Caroline looked at him and then at her mother, but she didn't say anything and Wally knew why. If the girls squealed, the boys would tell about the cake. Even-Steven.

Mrs. Malloy turned toward the house. "We have these to do," she said, "as well as the storm windows there in the garage. We might as well do them all."

Wally stared in dismay. There were twenty windows at least on the house, which meant twenty storm windows more stored in the garage. This time he heard a *definite* snicker from the girls on the grass.

"The girls will help, of course," said their mother, and Caroline's smile disappeared in an instant. So did Beth's and Eddie's. "What you boys can do is get the ladder from the garage and soap each window. Eddie can turn the hose on them from below to rinse them, and you can dry them after that. Beth and Caroline will change the water whenever you need it, and get clean rags. With all seven of you working together, I doubt it should take more than a couple of hours. I'll have doughnuts and cider for you when you're done."

When Mrs. Malloy went inside for the bucket and rags, Jake looked over at Eddie: "Nice going." He smirked.

Eddie tossed her head and looked away.

▾ ▾ ▾

The old garage leaned a little to one side, but Wally didn't mind. It was his favorite place on the Bensons' property, and he and his brothers and the Benson boys used to play in there for hours. For a time they'd turned it into a club house, and other times it had become a hideout. It was dark and musty, with loose boards that creaked in the wind.

He and Jake carried the ladder from the garage and put it up to the first window of the house where Mrs. Malloy was pointing. Eddie glumly got out the hose, and after Mrs. Malloy supervised the cleaning of the first window, she went back inside.

"Which window is yours, Eddie?" Josh called down. "I'll be sure to leave lots of smudges on it."

"Har, har," said Eddie.

The reason the work went so quickly was because no one spoke much after that. Wally had read once about an order of monks who went about their work in silence and never spoke except for one hour on Friday evenings. This must be what it was like to be a monk, he decided as he carried the last of the storm windows out of the garage, except that there wouldn't be any girl monks around.

Josh did the climbing of the ladder, Beth kept him supplied with clean water and rags, Jake and Wally carried storm windows in and out of the garage, Eddie hosed them off, and Caroline and Peter wiped the storm windows clean. In and out, up and down, back and forth. . . .

Mrs. Malloy had been right about one thing—the work *did* go faster with so many of them helping. Once, as he passed Caroline, she looked so cheerful, he was about to tell *her* about the monks who never talked except for an hour on Friday evenings, but then he remembered she was the enemy, so he told Jake instead.

"If there were girl monks, you know what they'd be called?" he asked, grinning. "Monk-ees."

Jake laughed out loud.

It was then that it happened, but no one knew quite how. It might have been Jake's laugh that made Eddie turn, hose in hand, but as she did, the water made a loop in the air and caught Josh, up on the ladder. His bucket came crashing to the ground with a splash, two inches away from Beth, soaking her to the skin with brown, dirty water.

While Wally stared, Beth pushed a sponge in Jake's face, Peter rushed to help his brother, Caroline went to help her sisters, and Wally simply tried to get the hose out of Eddie's hand. It was spewing water in every direction. The next great battle of the war had begun.

"Hey, what's this?" cried Mrs. Malloy, coming out of the house. "Girls! Stop it!"

Wally, who had the hose now, was holding it upright like a pitchfork, and realized that water was cascading down onto Mrs. Malloy's flower bed. As he jerked it away, he sent a stream of water across the porch, catching the girls' mother right in the face.

Wally gasped.

Spluttering, Mrs. Malloy rushed down the steps and turned off the faucet, then stood there shaking water from her clothes.

"Now, what's this all about?" she demanded.

"They started it, Mom," said Caroline, wringing out the tail of her shirt.

"We did not!" said Jake hotly. "Eddie turned the hose on Josh."

"He dropped his bucket on purpose!" cried Beth.

"I did not!" said Josh.

Mrs. Malloy looked around curiously. "You kids hardly know each other! How did you get to be enemies so soon?"

Wally looked at Caroline. *I dare you,* his eyes told her. No one spoke for a moment.

"Just fooling around, Mom," said Caroline.

"Yeah, just goofing off," Eddie murmured.

"Nobody's hurt," added Beth.

"Well, let's finish up that last window, then, and have some refreshment," Mrs. Malloy said.

For a moment they all looked as though they were going to laugh, Wally thought. They *did* look funny, with their heads dripping water, their clothes soaking wet. And when Mrs. Malloy brought out the doughnuts and cider, and they sat on the steps to eat, he thought, for maybe one fifth of a second, that the war might be over.

That was before Mrs. Malloy went back inside, however. That was before the boys started home. Because they had not gone ten feet from the house when suddenly, *Bam! Pow! Biff! Splatt!*

Two wet rags and two soggy sponges hit the boys on the backs of their necks, and when Wally and his brothers wheeled around, the Malloy girls were disappearing inside the house and the door slammed shut.

"That does it," said Jake. "We've got to do something. What's the scariest thing you can think of, Wally? We'll start with Beth. Have you thought of anything yet?"

And, as always, Wally said the first thing that came to mind: "Floating heads."

"Like we used to do with the Bensons on Halloween?" said Jake, his eyes lighting up. "Wally, it's wonderful! It's perfect!"

"Floating heads!" said Josh.

"Wow!" breathed Peter.

Eight

Floating Heads

It was almost too delicious to think about. All through dinner that evening Wally tried not to smile, but whenever he caught Josh's or Jake's eye, he felt the corners of his mouth turning up just a bit at the edges.

"Well, how did the window cleaning go?" Mr. Hatford asked as he passed the peas.

"Went okay," said Josh.

"Did you get better acquainted with the Malloy girls?" asked their mother. "What are they like?"

"A Whomper, a Weirdo, and a Crazie," replied Peter.

"Just girls, Mom, that's all," Wally said quickly.

Mrs. Hatford helped herself to the ravioli in the center of the table. "Did Mrs. Malloy say anything more about my cake?"

"No. . . ."

Mom looked disappointed, Wally thought.

There was a little framed motto on the wall of the dining room: *If Mama ain't happy, ain't nobody happy,* it said. Maybe that was true of the Malloys as well. If the Malloy girls were unhappy here in Buckman, their mother wouldn't be happy either. And if Mrs. Malloy wasn't happy, she'd probably talk her husband into taking them back to Ohio. Wally hoped so, anyway.

But right now it was Mrs. Hatford who was unhappy.

"I had rather hoped—well, a cake like that wins ribbons in some places!" she said.

"First time you see her, she'll probably ask for the recipe," said Father. "*Nobody* makes chocolate chiffon cake the way you do, Ellen."

Wally went back to studying the ravioli on his plate. It was only recently Mother had tried anything fancy like ravioli. Usually, the people of Buckman stuck to fried chicken, beef pot-roasts, and pork chops with gravy. But someone had told Mrs. Hatford about the frozen ravioli you could buy at the grocery, and Wally was trying to figure out how they got the meat inside the little squares of dough. Did they make a pocket of dough first and then cut a little hole in the top and pour in the filling? Or did they put the meat between two pieces of dough, like a sandwich, and seal the edges together, or—

"Eat, Wally," said his father.

Wally quit studying the ravioli and thought about floating heads again. Last year at Halloween, when the Bensons were still here, the boys had frightened the residents of Buckman half to death with their floating heads.

It was the Bensons' idea, actually. Each boy bought a rubber mask, the scariest he could find, and each set out with a flashlight, long after tricks-or-treats were over for the evening, when children were settling down to count the pieces of candy they had collected and adults were turning off porch lights, glad that another Halloween was over. What each Benson and Hatford boy had done was sneak up to a lighted window, rap on the pane, then hold a flashlight beneath his chin so that the light illuminated the rubber mask and no more.

To a child looking up, or an adult turning around in his or her chair, all that could be seen in the dark outside was a grotesque head, made worse by the fact that the boy did not just stand there, but bobbed up and down, this way and that, so that it seemed for all the world as if a bodiless head were floating around outside the window. Children screeched, women screamed, and by the time anyone got to the door, the boys were halfway down the street, laughing to beat the band.

Jake had planned the details. They would wait until later, when Mother was working on her quilt and Dad was watching TV. Then they would creep outside with the zombie mask from last year, the worst of the lot, quietly place the ladder against the Malloys' house, just beneath Beth's window, and

Josh would climb up with the mask and flashlight, and rap.

"I know which window it is too," Josh had said. "When I was washing the windows, I found out where each girl sleeps. Eddie's got baseball stuff all over her walls, Caroline's got pictures of movie stars, and Beth's got books."

He sat down to draw a picture of Beth throwing up her hands in fright as she stared at a face outside her window. Josh had four sketchbooks full of drawings of all that the Hatfords had done with the Bensons when they lived in Buckman, and one of the favorite ways to spend a rainy day was to get out the sketches and remember how and where they had done each thing. Already, the boys discovered, Jake had a sketch of what Caroline might have looked like had she been eaten by fish, a picture of Eddie dumping her tray over Jake's head in the cafeteria, a sketch of the girls in the river trying to retrieve the plate, and a drawing of the girls and their mother right after the water fight.

Peter grinned as he studied the picture of Beth and the floating head. "Make her mouth open and her eyes look like *this*!" he said, demonstrating.

▼ ▼ ▼

After dinner the boys were strangely quiet, sitting around the living room pretending to watch TV with their father, their eyes on the clock. Sometimes Mr. Hatford fell asleep on the couch and slept right up until bedtime. Then he wouldn't know whether the boys were home or not. They could leave the TV on, and Mother, stitching her quilt upstairs, would think they were all in the living room.

To Wally's horror, however, Father suddenly reached over, turned off the TV, and stretched.

"Same old stuff, night after night," he said. "One of these evenings I think I'd like to walk over to the college and watch football practice—see what kind of a team we've got shaping up this year."

Jake and Josh exchanged glances.

"You'd have to go early, Dad, because I think they only practice until six-thirty," Wally said.

"I know. Maybe tomorrow. Think I'll go outside awhile, stretch my legs." He got up, put on a jacket, and went out on the porch.

"Hoo boy," said Josh. The boys followed him out, and walked beside him as he sauntered along the river.

"My favorite season," he said. "Used to walk along this very same path when I was just a little kid. Spent my whole life in this town, you know that?"

"Did you ever want to live anywhere else?" asked Wally.

"Noplace I could think of."

"So why did the Bensons leave?" asked Jake. "We thought *they* liked it here too."

"Hal Benson just wanted to try out another college—see if he liked teaching down in Georgia as much as he liked the school up here. Guess you have to try something to be sure." Father looked down at Wally, who was on his left side. "You miss those boys, don't you?"

"What do you think?" said Wally.

"Don't you figure it might be kinda fun to have a mess of girls around for a while?"

"You're joking," said Josh.

Even in the darkness Wally could tell that his dad was grinning a little. "I don't know, that young one's kind of cute. Something's a little wrong with her nose, though. Don't quite know what it is."

▼ ▼ ▼

About nine o'clock, Father was in the cellar, using the electric sander on an old dresser Mother wanted refinished, and she was upstairs working on her quilt, the radio going beside her.

Peter was supposed to have had his bath and be in bed, but because the boys had promised, they agreed to take him with them if they could get him out of the house unseen.

"We're going down to the bridge, Mom," Wally called to his mother. "Be back in a little while."

"Don't you go picking up poison ivy, now," Mrs. Hatford called, trying to hold a needle between her lips as she spoke, then running it through the quilt again.

"We won't. We'll stay on the path," Wally said.

There was no answer. Mother was humming along with the radio.

"C'mon," Wally whispered into Peter's room,

and the small boy tiptoed after them, his untied sneakers sticking out below his pajama bottoms.

They whispered all the way across the bridge, even though they didn't have to be quiet there. By the time they got to Island Avenue on the other side, they weren't saying anything at all. Josh had the green zombie mask with the gray eyes, Jake had the flashlight, and Wally and Peter were going along as lookouts.

It was a good thing the Malloys didn't have any dogs, Wally thought, because a dog would have heard them coming as soon as they crossed the bridge. As it was the boys kept to the shadows, and all strained to see if there was a light on in the right-hand bedroom above the front porch—Beth's room. There was. Wally and Jake poked each other and grinned. They crept up the side of the Malloys' driveway and opened the door of the garage.

Squeeeak! They froze in their tracks. All faces turned toward the house. But no one appeared at the windows, no one came to the door, and at last, convinced they were undetected, they picked up the long ladder, Wally at one end, Jake at the other, and carried it silently over to the bedroom in the corner.

Again they watched. Again they waited. Still no one came.

"Ready?" Jake whispered.

Josh nodded and slipped on the zombie mask. Wally sucked in his breath.

Flashlight in hand, Josh started up the rungs.

He was going as quietly as he could, Wally could tell, but even then the ladder seemed to make a kind of *pung, pung* sound with each step.

"Shhhh," warned Jake below. Josh stopped and waited. Nobody came. He went on.

Wally and his brothers watched. Josh stopped and adjusted the mask. He went up two more rungs until he was right outside Beth's window. At that very minute the light inside went out. And a second later, Josh's flashlight came on. He tapped, then bobbed up and down, this way and that.

There was a scream from inside—a cross between a train whistle and a fire alarm.

Whipping off his mask, Josh came down the ladder two rungs at a time.

They could hear Mr. Malloy yelling, "Beth? What's wrong?" Footsteps. More yelling. Voices.

The boys sprinted back down the driveway, watching the house over their shoulders. Wally faced forward again to see a baseball cap coming toward them, but there was no time to prevent a collision.

Wham! Crunch!

"Going somewhere?" came Eddie's voice.

"Yikes!" hollered Wally as a hand grabbed his shirt. He had never known that a tall, skinny girl could be so strong. She seemed to have Josh by the collar as well, dragging them both back toward the house. Wally wrestled free, but collided again, this time with Jake, and then he tripped over Peter. In the dark it was hard to see which arm belonged to whom.

"What are you guys up to anyway?" asked Eddie, but the boys got away and ran pell-mell to the bridge.

"You got the flashlight?" Jake asked Wally breathlessly.

"Heck, no. You were carrying it."

"I thought you grabbed it," Josh said. *"Someone did!"*

But that someone was already inside the house.

Nine

Ransom

Caroline was standing in the bathroom, practicing expressions in the mirror. She had actually been studying her eyebrows to see what they did when she went from sad to frightened, from scared to angry, and it was then she heard the scream.

Thinking her sister was being strangled, Caroline rushed into the room across the hall to find Beth on the floor, her chair overturned, eyes huge.

"What *is* it?" Caroline cried.

"Oh, Caroline, the most horrible thing right outside my window!"

"Girls, what's going on?" asked their father, hurrying in. Mother followed.

"Dad, there was something right outside my window!" Beth cried, still shaken.

"What was it?"

"A bobbing head. A floating face! It was green

with gray eyes, and . . . oh, it was awful! All decayed, with drool coming out of its mouth, and . . ."

Father reached down and picked up the book Beth had been reading: *The Creeping Dead.*

"Don't you think it's time you read something else for a change?"

"I only had half a chapter to go, and I just had to know how it ended," Beth said. "But what I saw wasn't my imagination; it was real!"

Caroline and her mother went to the window.

"Well, I don't see a thing," said Mrs. Malloy. "Eddie went next door to take back the eggs I borrowed. I'll bet it was her."

"It wasn't Eddie!" Beth declared.

"I'll go check," said Father.

He started down the stairs, the others behind him, just as Eddie came up.

"What's happening?" she asked.

"You missed a floating face," Caroline told her dryly. "Dad's going out to check."

"Don't bother," Eddie said. "Guess who I just bumped into? Crashed into, actually, they were in such a hurry to get away."

"Them?" cried Beth.

Eddie nodded.

"Who?" said Mother. "Those Hatford boys?"

"The very same," said Eddie. "There's a ladder up against the house, right under Beth's window."

"What now!" Mother exclaimed. "Those guys must drive their mother nuts."

Coach Malloy, however, was grinning. "That's the kind of thing you get when you have boys, Jean. Now, don't you go telling on them. They helped wash our windows, didn't they?"

Caroline waited as her parents went back downstairs, then she and Eddie went inside Beth's bedroom and shut the door.

"Those guys are terrible!" Beth said angrily.

"It could have been worse," said Caroline. "You could have been naked." Frankly, it had been a wonderful trick, Caroline decided, and she only wished that she had thought of it first to play on the boys.

"We've got to get even!" Beth declared. "We've just *got* to, Eddie!"

Eddie only smiled. "We already have. I've got their flashlight. A *good* flashlight too. I'll bet it belongs to their dad. They won't get it back unless they give us something in return."

"What?" asked Caroline.

"I haven't decided yet," said Eddie. "But believe me, they'll have to crawl!"

It would make such a marvelous story, Caroline thought. Sort of like Cinderella, only with the shoe on the other foot. This time *they* had the glass slipper, and whoever it belonged to had to come beg for it.

▼ ▼ ▼

On their way to school the next day Beth and Eddie showed Caroline the ransom note they had written to the Hatfords:

To whom it may concern:

If you ever hope to see your flashlight again, you will meet us at the swinging bridge at 7:30 this evening, and you will each say aloud, "I am honestly and truly sorry for the trouble I have caused, and will be a faithful, obedient servant of the realm, now and forever."

The Malloy Musketeers

"Servant of the realm?" Caroline asked. "What does that mean?"

"I don't know," said Beth, "but I read it in a book, and it sounded wonderful."

"It *is* wonderful!" said Caroline. "We could go walking down the path tonight single file, dressed like Egyptian princesses or something, and make them kneel down on one knee when they said it."

"Not me," said Eddie. "I'm not going as any princess."

"The boys would never do that," said Beth. "Getting them to say they're sorry is going to be hard enough."

"Who gets the note?" Caroline wanted to know.

"You're going to give it to Wally. If we gave it to

Jake or Josh, they wouldn't even read it—probably just make a spitball out of it," Eddie said.

Caroline could hardly wait to get to class. When the bell rang and she went in her room, however, Wally wouldn't even look at her, which told her just how upset the boys were that they had lost their father's flashlight.

She decided to wait until Miss Applebaum finished talking before she dropped the note over Wally's shoulder. But Miss Applebaum wouldn't shut up. She was talking about the invention of the telegraph or something, which did not interest Caroline in the least. Caroline rested her head on one hand and drew a picture of Miss Applebaum in her notebook.

The more the teacher droned on, the wilder the drawing became. She gave Miss Applebaum a monstrous mouth, with fire coming out of it. She gave her horns and a tail and scales like a dragon. The dragon lady even looked like Miss Applebaum—had the same kind of hair and the same kind of glasses. Clickety, clackety went the teacher's mouth, like a telegraph of its own.

Wally raised one hand to go to the bathroom and Miss Applebaum nodded that he could go.

Now, thought Caroline, while he was out of the room. She waited until Miss Applebaum was looking the other way, then quickly leaned forward and dropped the note onto Wally's desk.

When Wally came back, Miss Applebaum was

still carrying on, and Caroline was busily drawing claws on the teacher's hands and feet.

She saw Wally's head bend down over the desk as though he were looking at something, saw his arms move slightly as though he were unfolding a piece of paper, and then she watched as his ears turned from pink to red.

A few minutes later a small piece of paper came flying over Wally's shoulder and landed on her notebook. Caroline opened it.

Malloy Musketeers, it said. *Drop dead.*

The telegraph led to the telephone and the phonograph, and Caroline felt that she could not stand it another minute. This time *she* raised her hand to be allowed to go to the rest room, and when the teacher nodded, she tiptoed out. Once in the hallway she gave a big sigh of relief.

The girls' rest room was on the other side of the auditorium, and Caroline did a risky thing. Instead of going around she opened one of the great doors to the darkened room, took the four steps up onstage, and walked out to the middle, staring up at the rows of seats before her. Goose bumps rose on her arms.

Someday, she was sure, she would be here, with lights shining down on her, in a gorgeous costume, and she would dazzle the people of Buckman as they'd never been dazzled before. She walked to the very edge of the stage and whispered to the audience, "A faithful and obedient servant of the realm, now and forever." It sounded wonderfully mysterious and romantic. That done, she crossed over, went down the steps, and out the door on the other side.

All heads were bent over desks when Caroline came back into the room, and as she went down the aisle to her seat, Miss Applebaum said, "We are all writing a paragraph about what we think is the world's greatest invention, Caroline."

Thank goodness the lecture was over, Caroline thought, and reached for her pencil.

When she looked down at her notebook, however, she realized that the picture of Miss Applebaum was gone. There were little bits of paper around the three metal rings, as though a paper had been quickly snatched away. Her heart leapt. She stared up at the teacher, wondering if Miss Applebaum had come by and taken it.

But the teacher seemed completely undisturbed. Caroline stared at the back of Wally's head. *He* had taken it! He *must* have. When he came back from the rest room and walked by her desk, he must have seen what she was drawing. And somehow, when she was out of the room herself, he had managed to turn around and take the drawing.

When the papers were collected fifteen minutes later, Caroline was not even sure what she had written. And on the way out the door to recess, she poked Wally in the back. "You give me my paper or else," she said angrily.

Wally just smiled. "Meet me at the swinging bridge at seven-thirty this evening, and crawl down the path on your hands and knees," he said, and headed for the door.

Caroline was beside herself. This was blackmail! Beth and Eddie would never forgive her for doing something so stupid.

It was a horrible day, and as soon as school was out, Caroline charged out the door like a hornet and told Eddie and Beth what had happened. The Hatford boys had already headed for home, and were looking at the girls over their shoulders, laughing and hooting as they went.

When Caroline and her sisters reached the swinging bridge, Caroline was too angry to go home. Too angry to speak, almost. She stood glaring after the Hatford boys as they went up on the porch of their house and slammed the door. And then she saw something else: clothes drying on the clothesline in back of their house.

"Wait here," she told Beth and Eddie.

She marched right up on the Hatfords' lawn. Without looking to the right or left she stalked around to the back, grabbed a pair of Jockey shorts off the clothesline, then ran for her life as the boys came out on the porch and stared.

Waving the Jockey shorts high in the air, she tore across the swinging bridge, Beth and Eddie behind her, and didn't stop until they were safely in their house and up in Caroline's room.

"Wonderful!" said Eddie.

"I'll show them all around school!" Caroline declared. "I'll tell everyone in my class they're Wally's. 'How are your Munsingwears today?' I'll ask him. He and his brothers don't get back their flashlight *or* shorts until they return my drawing of Miss Applebaum *and* get down on one knee and apologize."

The phone rang.

"I'll bet they want to exchange things right now," Beth said, giggling, as the girls dashed out in the hall. "They can't even wait until evening."

Caroline picked up the phone. "Malloy Musketeers, Caroline speaking."

There was a short pause at the other end. And then a man's voice said, "Caroline, this is Mr. Hatford, across the river. I wonder if you would mind returning my briefs."

Ten

Siren Song

Wally, Josh, Jake, and Peter stood still as cement as their father made the phone call.

Mr. Hatford turned around, phone in hand.

"She says she'll return my briefs if you return her paper, Wally. Do you know what she's talking about?"

Wally nodded and swallowed. "Tell her I'll return the paper if she returns the flashlight."

Mr. Hatford spoke into the phone again. "He says he'll return the paper if you return the flashlight. Don't ask me what's going on around here. I'm only their father. . . . Okay, five minutes from now on the bridge. . . . He'll be there."

Wally's father put down the telephone and looked at the boys. "That wouldn't be *my* flashlight she's talking about, would it?"

Wally nodded still again.

"Is this what goes on in the afternoons when

I'm not here? People run off with my flashlight and shorts? I get home early for the first time in a couple of months, and what do I see? Some girl leaving our yard at sixty miles an hour waving my underwear in the wind!"

"She's the Crazie," Peter explained soberly.

"Well, if you've got something of hers, Wally, you get on out to the bridge and give it back. I want my briefs and my flashlight back, and anything else that's missing. What do they want next? Socks? Toothbrush? Keys? They holding a garage sale or something?"

Wally went to his room for Caroline's drawing of Miss Applebaum.

"You guys have to come too," he murmured to the others, and they all followed him out the door.

For a minute or so they trudged silently across the yard and over to the other side of the road.

"Once we get Dad's stuff back, we'll be even," Wally said, thinking that this would be a good time to forget about the Malloys once and for all.

"But we can't stop now!" said Jake. "If we're not bugging the girls, what *will* we do?"

That was something Wally hadn't thought about. "Mom will enroll us in violin lessons," he said worriedly.

"She'll make us get a paper route," said Josh.

"She'll send us to camp next summer," said Peter.

Jake grinned. "So we've got to stay busy, right?"

"Right," said Wally.

The boys looked at each other and smiled.

"Tell you what," said Josh. "We won't start anything if *they* don't."

"Yeah," said Jake. "But they will."

Caroline and her sisters were coming across the bridge. Wally knew that his dad was back on the porch watching, and he wasn't about to do anything dumb like float Caroline's paper over the edge of the cable railing.

Caroline's face was red. He had never seen her embarrassed before, but he was looking at it now.

"Here's your paper," he muttered.

"Here's your stuff," said Caroline, and handed him a sack.

Eddie and Beth looked daggers at all four boys together.

"You better check that sack," whispered Josh as the boys turned and started back again. "They probably took the batteries out of the flashlight."

Wally looked in the sack. Everything was there. He checked the flashlight. Two batteries, one bulb. He took out the briefs and turned them over. No writing on the seat of the pants.

"Thank you," said their father when they reached the porch. "Now, do you think it's possible that you boys can stay out of trouble for a couple of days? If you want something to do, you could wash *our* windows, not to mention my car or the dishes or the kitchen floor."

"I've got homework," said Jake.

"Me too," said Wally, and all four boys went upstairs.

▼ ▼ ▼

There was always a "Back-to-School" night in Buckman the second week of September. No matter what, every parent who had a child in school was supposed to go to his or her classroom that night, meet the teacher, sit in the kid's seat, and listen to a talk about what the students would be learning that year. Afterward there were cookies and coffee in the gym, and the principal went around shaking hands. You no more missed Back-to-School night in Buckman than you missed your grandmother's funeral.

Mr. Hatford was going to spend the evening in Josh and Jake's classroom, while Mrs. Hatford would divide the evening between Miss Applebaum and Peter's teacher. The boys, of course, would stay at home.

Always before, on Back-to-School night, the Hatfords went to the Bensons', or the Bensons came to the Hatfords', and the boys wrestled on the rug, made popcorn, ate candy, enjoying the fact that for once they were free and their folks were in school.

But this time there were no Bensons to come over, and to make matters worse, it rained.

"We could go through the kitchen and eat all the chocolate chips," said Wally.

"There aren't any, I already looked," Jake told him.

"We could call up some of the guys at school to come over," said Josh.

"Who do we like at school?" Jake asked. There were friends, of course, but none they liked as well as the Bensons.

"We could wrap up in blankets and roll down the stairs," said Peter.

"Negative," said Josh.

They decided at last to turn out all the lights and play hide and seek. Wally was it.

He sat down on the couch in the living room and counted to fifty.

"Here I come, ready or not," he yelled, and groped his way to the hall.

It was one of the most exciting games the boys played, and they reserved it for moments of incredible boredom. When you were "it" in the dark you never knew when a hand was going to reach out and grab you, whether you would crawl under the bed and find a body, whether you would collide with someone on the stairs.

He heard a soft thud from somewhere, but wasn't quite sure if it was up or down, in or out. It had to be in, though, because outside was off-limits. There were three live bodies waiting to be found, and in the dark, they could change hiding places as much as they liked. Even if you touched something, you had to make sure it was a person.

The noise came again. Upstairs. Wally was sure of that now. He ran his hand along the wall and started up, his other hand sweeping the air in front of him.

Halfway up the stairs, however, he heard another sound, and this time goose bumps rose on his arms. It was a sound like nothing he had ever heard before.

It seemed to be half human, half animal, yet more like a fire siren, only very, very soft. It rose and fell like the wind. Maybe it *was* the wind.

Then it stopped, and all Wally heard was the rain beating down on the roof. He went on, running his hand along the wall, poking each step with his foot to make sure there wasn't a hand ready to grab his ankle. Just as he got to the top, however, the strange siren song came again.

He heard somebody running along the hallway, and then Peter's voice, calling shakily, "Wally?"

"What's the matter?" Wally said, putting out his other hand so Peter wouldn't run into him. Peter ran into him anyway, and grabbed his arm.

"What's that noise?" Peter said.

"I don't know. Probably Jake or Josh."

"I don't wanna play this game anymore," Peter told him.

"Well, go down and sit on the couch, then, until I find the other guys."

"No, I wanna stay by you."

Whoooeeeooo. Whoooeeeooo.

It was not a siren. It was not anything Wally could figure out.

"Josh, cut it out," he yelled.

"It's not me," came a voice from one of the bedrooms. "What the heck is it?"

"Jake, I'll bet."

"Turn on the lights," Peter begged.

"No, we can't until we find Jake. That's the rule."

Whoooeee, whoooeee, whoooeeeoooo. . . .

Footsteps downstairs.

"Hey, what are you guys doing?" came Jake's voice. "Who's singing that song?"

It was *not* Jake. Three sets of feet went flying down the stairs, the boys tumbling and rolling, until Wally and his brothers lay in a heap at the bottom.

Eleven

Trapped

Three figures huddled on the widow's walk on top of the Hatfords' house. Rain beat steadily down on their yellow slickers and the air was cold.

"Even if we catch pneumonia and die, it's worth it," said Caroline, her teeth chattering.

"Even if we fall off the roof and break both legs," Eddie agreed.

"One more time?" Beth asked.

"No. Didn't you hear them running? Let's wait until we think they've forgotten about it, then sock it to them again," said Eddie. They giggled.

It had all started when Beth heard a group of women called Sweet Honey in the Rock on the radio, singing a song they had written called "Emergency." She had called the others to listen. Caroline wasn't sure how they did it, but, using only their voices, the singers had managed to make themselves sound just like a fire siren, each singing a different pitch, but rising and falling together at exactly the same time.

So Caroline, Beth, and Eddie had gone out in the garage and lain in the loft, practicing quietly, and they did it—not as well as Sweet Honey in the Rock, but well enough. What's more, they discovered that if they kept their voices soft, and wavered them just a little, they sounded like something none of them had ever heard before—not a siren, exactly—not quite human, not quite animal. . . . And as soon as they discovered that, they knew what they were going to do. Never had they felt such power.

"How long should we wait? I'm so soggy, I'm going to grow mushrooms," Beth said.

"We have to lull them into thinking they were imagining things," Eddie told her.

Caroline smiled to herself in the dark as she huddled in her corner of the widow's walk. She had been so embarrassed when Mr. Hatford called and asked for his briefs back! And then, to have to walk down to the bridge with Mr. Hatford watching, and exchange things with Wally—it was too much; a humiliation that dreadful needed revenge.

She almost wished it were daylight and clear so that she could see out over Buckman. It felt strange being up here on the Hatfords' roof at night, and she imagined how much fun the boys must have had spying on her and her sisters when her family first moved in. If she and Eddie and Beth had lived over here, and it were the *Hatfords* moving in, she had no doubt they would have been spying on *them*. But that was beside the point. She wasn't even sure *what* the point was anymore, except that she and Beth and Eddie had never had so much excitement back in Ohio, and she hoped they would not go back when a year was over.

"Okay, let's do it again," Eddie whispered.

All three girls leaned down over the trapdoor in the roof, mouths close against the crack.

"One, two, three . . . go," said Beth.

And then they sang the song—the terrible, electrifying siren song that started low and soft, then rose higher and higher, louder and louder, tapering off into nothing, like the wind.

There was the thud of running feet once more from inside. Closet doors opening and closing. Yells. Squares of yellow light appeared on the lawn as lights went on all over the house.

"We're driving them absolutely nuts." Eddie grinned.

"Positively bonkers," said Caroline. "How long are we going to keep doing this? Till they come running and screaming out of the house with their hands up?"

It was a question they hadn't discussed.

"Why don't we keep it up till their parents get home?" said Beth.

"Because then *our* parents will be home, and we'll have a lot of explaining to do," said Eddie.

"What time is it?"

Eddie tried to see her watch in the darkness. "Eight-thirty, I think."

"Fifteen more minutes, then," Caroline said. "Mom said not to expect them back before nine. That will give us time to get home and put the ladder away."

The footsteps and door banging went on for some time before the house grew quiet again. Once more Beth gave the signal, and once more the three girls leaned over, noses almost touching the roof, and made the sound that rose and fell like the wind. This time they wavered their voices, so that the song was even more eerie—ghostlike.

When they stopped, however, there was no noise from below. No voices, no footsteps. Nothing. The girls did it again, a little louder, and waited. Still nothing. Caroline looked over the side of the railing. There were no squares of yellow light on the lawn, meaning that the boys had turned out all the lights. What were they doing?

She and Eddie and Beth exchanged glances.

"Maybe they left. Maybe they just silently closed up and headed for the school to get their parents," said Beth.

"Wouldn't that be a *blast*!" said Eddie.

"We could do this again sometime, when their folks are away," Beth laughed. "We could drive them *wild*."

"We could drive *them* out of Buckman, and

then we'd have the town to ourselves," said Caroline.

They waited a few minutes longer. If the boys *had* gone to the school to get their parents, it meant the Hatfords' car could be turning in at any moment.

"We'd better go," said Eddie.

Carefully they climbed over the side of the widow's walk, then made their way down the sloping roof, scooting along on the seat of their pants—slowly, cautiously, grasping the shingles with their fingertips as they came, Caroline in the lead. But when she reached the place they had left the ladder, Caroline saw that the ladder was gone.

"WHOEEEOOO!" came a yell from the yard below, and the four Hatford brothers emerged from the porch, yelling like banshees in the darkness.

For the second time Caroline's face burned with humiliation. There was nothing left but surrender.

"Okay, okay, put the ladder back up," she said, but the boys paid no attention.

"WHOEEEOOOO!" they yelped, running about the yard in the rain.

"Put that ladder back up!" Eddie commanded, as though it would do any good.

"You wanted to be up there, you're up there," yelled Jake. "Have a good time."

"Want some pillows? Have a good sleep!" called Josh.

It was beginning to rain harder now. It came

down in huge drops, like water splashing out of a basin.

"Wally!" bellowed Caroline, but the boys only laughed and ducked under the porch roof. What had been fun before was scary now. Because of the rain and the dark, it was hard to maneuver.

"Come on," said Beth, inching her way back up the roof. "I've got an idea."

Caroline and Eddie followed clumsily, strands of wet hair blowing in their faces. Caroline felt wet through and through. They reached the railing around the widow's walk and crawled under.

"I just have a hunch. . . ." Beth said, bending over the trapdoor again. "Help me lift it, Eddie. See if it's latched."

All three girls edged their fingers beneath the rim of the lid to the trapdoor and tugged. Just as Beth suspected, the boys hadn't latched it again after their last spying episode.

The girls stared down into total darkness.

"Are there stairs?" Eddie asked.

Caroline leaned over and put one arm down as far as it would reach. "No," she said disappointedly.

"We could jump," said Eddie.

"We don't dare. We don't know what's under there."

"What good is this going to do?" Eddie said.

"Just wait," Beth told her. "We're going to keep the door open. You'll see."

There was hail along with the rain now—smaller stones at first, then larger and larger.

"WHOOOOEEEEOOOO!" yelled the boys delightedly on the porch below.

"Let's go inside where it's warm and dry," came Jake's voice loudly from the porch.

"Yeah, let's make some hot chocolate," said Wally.

"With marshmallows," added Peter. "Yum, yum!"

There was the sound of a door slamming as the boys went back in.

A minute went by. Then two or three. The rain and hail was hitting the floor beneath the trapdoor. The girls could hear it.

Suddenly a light came on, illuminating the Hatfords' attic and the stepladder beneath. Hail was pinging against the floor. There was already a large puddle of water.

"Hey!" came Wally's voice. "Jake! They've opened the trap! They're letting in water!"

Feet pounded on the stairs, and Caroline looked down into Josh's and Jake's angry faces.

"Close the trap!" Jake demanded. "You'll ruin the floor."

"So?" said Caroline.

A car was pulling in the driveway.

"Your folks are home," said Eddie.

"Come on down! Get out of here! Hurry up!" Josh yelled.

Caroline slid inside, holding on to the raised edge around the opening of the trap until her feet were securely on top of the stepladder. Eddie came next, and finally Beth, pulling the door closed behind her.

"Hurry!" Josh was saying, pushing them toward the stairs to the second floor, and they thundered down, the boys at their heels.

But it was too late. Just as Caroline reached the front door, it opened, and Mr. and Mrs. Hatford walked in.

"Hello," said Caroline, and then, as she and her sisters went outside, "Good-bye."

Twelve

Letters

Mr. Hatford looked at his wife.

"Was it just my imagination, or did I see three girls, in yellow raincoats, walk out our front door?"

"You did," said Wally's mother. "Listen, you guys, what in the world is going on?"

"Those girls were up on our roof," Wally said.

"In *this* rain?"

"They were, Mom," Josh put in.

"Singing!" added Peter, nodding his head.

Mr. Hatford looked slowly around the room. "Singing in the rain; three girls in yellow raincoats; nine o'clock at night; on the roof."

"How did they get up there?" asked Mother.

"They brought a ladder," said Peter.

Wally wished his younger brother hadn't said that, because he knew what the next question would be. It was his father who asked and answered it both.

"If they got *up* the ladder to get to the roof, why didn't they go *down* the ladder to get to the ground? Because the boys took the ladder away, why else?"

Wally wanted to sneak off to the living room with his brothers, but Father was in the doorway.

Mother sighed. "I used to think the Benson boys were more than I could take, but those girls are going to drive me wild. I wonder if the Malloys give any thought at all to how they are raising their children."

"Now, Ellen, we saw George and Jean Malloy at the school tonight, and they seemed warm and friendly to me," Father told her.

"Not friendly enough to tell me they liked my cake," Mother said huffily. "I gave them every opportunity, and all they talked about was how nice it was for the boys to wash their windows." She took off her jacket and hung it up. "Even sent the plate back without anything on it, a crack in it too. That's just not the way we do things in Buckman."

Wally ducked sheepishly under his father's arm and made his escape.

A letter arrived the following day from the Benson boys addressed to J.J.W. and P. Hatford:

Hi, Guys!

It's raining down here, so we figured it was time to write you all a letter. How ya doing?

We're doing okay, I guess. You know what Georgia's full of? Red ants. Red ants and roaches and lots of peach and pecan trees, and, of course, sun.

We've got this big old house—really, really old—near the University, and so far Dad likes it here. Mom too. She likes this house. It's got this enormous attic you wouldn't believe. If you guys were down here we'd be up in the attic all the time, I'll bet. Stuff's hidden in the walls—old newspapers and things, I mean. One of them dates back to 1887. Mom said the house used to belong to a Confederate soldier. We've been looking for bullets and stuff at the back of the yard, but so far we haven't found any.

Did Wally get Applebaum this year? You should see the teacher Danny got. A Georgia P-E-A-C-H. Every guy who gets her this year is one lucky stiff. School's not too bad. Lots of boys here, right in our neighborhood, too, so that's good. Wish you were here, though.

The first thing we'd do if you ever come down to Georgia is go up to the attic, because it's probably the first thing you'd want to see.

The second thing would be to ride around town on the tour bus. Boy, there's so much to do you could probably live here twenty years and not do it all.

Anyway, write to us sometime and tell us about the people who moved into our house. Mom wants to know if they're taking good care of it. I asked her the other day if we were going back to Buckman after the year is up, and she said she didn't know, it was up to Dad. So I asked him, and he said, "Who knows?"

Take care, you guys,
Bill
(and Danny and Steve and Tony and Doug)

Dear Bill (and Danny and Steve and Tony and Doug):

We got your letter and I can't say we're glad you like Georgia, because we hoped you wouldn't. You want to know who rents your house? A Whomper, a Weirdo, and a Crazie, that's who. So far here is what these girls have done:

1. Outpitched the boys at recess (even Jake).

2. Pretended one of their sisters (the Crazie) was dead and dumped her in the river.

3. Threw a cake in the river.

4. Stole a flashlight.

5. Stole Dad's underwear.

6. Crawled up on our roof in a rainstorm and hollered through our trapdoor.

If you were here, and we were in Georgia, would you be glad? I don't care if you guys have a Georgia P-E-A-C-H for a teacher or not. I don't care if you have Miss America. If you don't come back and send these dweebs back to Ohio, I'll tell everyone in Buckman how you wet your pants once on the playground.

Wally
(and Jake and Josh and Peter)

P.S. I don't know if the Malloys are taking good care

of your house or not. We had to go over and wash their windows for them. That should tell you something.

"I'll bet they're never coming back," Wally said as he sealed his letter.

"They sure didn't sound very sad about being in Georgia," said Josh.

"You know what?" said Jake after a minute. "If one of the Malloy girls ever comes over here again, let's kidnap her. Lock her up. We'll make her sisters pay plenty to get her back."

"Wow!" said Peter.

Thirteen

Kidnapped

"Tom and Ellen Hatford seem like such nice people," Mother said at breakfast as she put some melon on the table. "Did I tell you girls that we talked with them a little while at the school the other night? I told them I appreciated the boys helping wash our windows."

"Yeah, great job," Eddie said dryly.

"Mrs. Hatford, though, is . . . well, a bit on the odd side. I was standing with her over by the refreshment table, and as I reached for a cookie, she said she was glad my family enjoyed desserts so much, that we all had such hearty appetites. One little cookie, and she made it sound as though the five of us could finish off a whole cake in one meal! Strange."

"Very," agreed Eddie.

At school that morning Caroline did not cross the auditorium to get to the rest room as she had been doing once a day since she had discovered the new route. The sixth-graders were in the auditorium watching a film, so it was not till lunchtime that, when Caroline peeked, it was dark and empty once again.

She did not have any trouble finding opportunities to step up on the stage. She could count on being excused from class at least once a day to go to the rest room. Sometimes she came in the building at recess to get a drink, and made an auditorium detour going back out again. If all else failed, she hurriedly ate her lunch and then—when she took her milk carton to the trash—simply walked on out the door into the hall, slipped into the auditorium, and, when she was finished, out the other side and onto the playground.

She'd gotten into the habit of taking a book in with her, any book at all, so she could practice reading a few paragraphs, with expression, from the stage. She could not talk nearly as loud as she would have liked, of course, because someone outside might hear, so she stage-whispered the paragraphs, always choosing a selection where at least two different people were speaking, to give her practice reading several parts.

The day before, she had read a selection from *Charlotte's Web,* where the spider confessed to eating other insects:

". . . I have to live, don't I?"

"Why, yes, of course," said Wilbur. "Do they taste good?"

"Delicious. Of course, I don't really eat them. I drink them—drink their blood. I love blood," said Charlotte, and her pleasant, thin voice grew even thinner and more pleasant.

Caroline had loved playing the part of Charlotte, and had practiced hard to make her voice "thin and pleasant." Pleasant was easy enough to do, but she'd had to work some to make it sound thin. The day before that she had read from *Alice in Wonderland:*

"But I don't want to go among mad people," Alice remarked.

"Oh, you can't help that," said the Cat: "we're all mad here. I'm mad. You're mad."

"How do you know I'm mad?" said Alice.

"You must be," said the Cat, "or you wouldn't have come here."

When she had found that passage in the book, she had thought all morning about how she should read the part of the Cheshire Cat. But today she had chosen a page from *The Wind in the Willows,* because it said that Mole spoke "in anguish of heart." All during arithmetic that morning she had wondered what sort of an expression "anguish of heart" would be. Something very dramatic, she was sure—a mixture of fear and sorrow, perhaps.

So when she went to throw out her milk carton in the trash after eating, she sneaked across the hall to the auditorium and, with the book tucked under her shirt, slipped up onstage, out from behind the thick velvet curtain, and directly to the center of the platform.

This was a conversation between Ratty and Mole. Caroline decided that she would look to the left when she was reading the part of Mole, and to the right when she was reading Ratty. She cleared her throat and began:

> The call was clear, the summons was plain. He must obey it instantly, and go. "Ratty!" he called, full of joyful excitement, "hold on! Come back! I want you quick!"
>
> "Oh, *come* along, Mole, do!" replied the Rat cheerfully, still plodding along.
>
> "Please stop, Ratty!" pleaded the poor Mole, in anguish of heart. "You don't understand! It's my home, my old home! I've just come across the smell of it, and it's close by here, really quite close. And I *must* go to it, I must, I must! Oh, come back, Ratty! Please, please come back!"

Caroline stiffled a sob.

There was a titter in the audience.

The audience?

Caroline's hand dropped, the book in it, and she stared hard into the darkness of the auditorium.

The laughter came again, louder this time, and quickly became a loud guffaw.

The next thing Caroline knew, Wally and some of the other fourth-grade boys were charging down the aisle and out the side door, yelling:

"Oh, please come back!"

"I *must* go, I *must*!"

And suddenly there was Miss Applebaum in the doorway, peering into the auditorium.

"Caroline?" she said.

Caroline walked stiffly offstage.

"What's going on in here?" the teacher asked. "You're supposed to be out on the playground."

"I was just leaving," Caroline said, and without looking in a mirror, she knew that her cheeks—her whole face, in fact—was flaming.

Out on the grass Wally and the other boys were doubled over. They reeled in laughter, fell against each other, and one boy lay on his back, screaming, "The smell of it! You don't understand! Oh, come back, Ratty! Please, please do!"

▼ ▼ ▼

Caroline did not tell her sisters what had happened in the auditorium. It was too embarrassing. They hadn't even known she was sneaking into the auditorium at all. She could think of nothing else the rest of the day, and wondered how long the boys had been there. It was Wally, she was sure, who had led them all there, but had they been spying on her at other times as well?

Had he been there the day she'd played tearful Becky Thatcher, lost in the cave with Tom Sawyer, and crying, *Tom, Tom, we're lost! we're lost!*

What she decided was that she would pay Wally back for this humiliation. This was a hundred times worse than stealing Mr. Hatford's shorts. Day in, day out, noontime, nighttime, she didn't care, somehow, someway, she would catch *him* doing something as embarrassing as being caught onstage had been for her.

For the next few days Caroline said nothing at all to Wally Hatford, but she scarcely took her eyes off him. She followed him at a distance on the playground at recess. She stared when he went to the front of the room to put a problem on the blackboard. She watched from the next table when he ate his lunch. One false move from Wally Hatford, and she'd never let him forget it.

Just let her catch him with something yucky between his teeth. Just let her catch him with his pants unzipped. Let her catch *him* drawing something crazy in his notebook. *Wally Hatford,* she recited every morning, *your time will come.*

▼ ▼ ▼

Sunday was a clear day, warm and dry, and on days like this, the Hatford boys usually played in their backyard after church, once their clothes were changed. Walking along the river, Caroline and her sisters had often seen them whooping it up, playing kickball or throwing horseshoes.

Mr. and Mrs. Malloy had left early that morning for the funeral of a friend back in Ohio, and wouldn't be home until night. Caroline realized that if she could hide herself somewhere near the Hatfords' house, she could spy on Wally all day without being missed. She told her sisters this much: "Wally embarrassed me awful in school on Friday, and I'm going to get back at him no matter what."

Beth was sprawled in a chair on the lawn reading *The Shadow of the Werewolf.* "Don't start anything till I finish this book," she said.

"Well, I'm taking lunch with me, and I may not be home for a long time," Caroline said. "I just wanted you to know."

"What have you got in the sack?"

"Marshmallows and cheese crackers."

"Toss me a marshmallow?" Beth said, holding out her hands, then popped it in her mouth and returned to her book.

Caroline set out just before the Hatfords were due home from church. She remembered having seen a shed in the back of their house when she had snatched Mr. Hatford's underwear from the line. This, she decided, was where she would hide, and had no trouble getting the door open and closing it after her.

Once inside, she wished she'd brought a pillow

or something, because the shed was dusty, with a bare earth floor, and crammed with hoes and shovels, lawn mower and sprinkler.

There was, however, a narrow space between the edge of the door where the hinges were and the rest of the shed, and Caroline found that by sitting on an old toolbox and putting her eye to the crack, she could see almost the entire yard.

The Hatfords' Chevy was just pulling into the driveway, and the boys got out and walked single-file to the house. They all looked stiff and weird in their Sunday shirts and ties, and Caroline smiled as she dug into her sack of cheese crackers, and settled herself more comfortably on the toolbox.

She had expected it would be an hour at least before the boys ate dinner and came out in the yard, but was surprised when Mr. and Mrs. Hatford stepped out instead, dressed in old clothes, and carrying some empty baskets.

"Are you *sure* you don't want to come to the orchard with us?" Mother said, turning to Wally and Josh in the doorway.

"No way!" Josh told her. "You pick the apples and we'll eat 'em."

"We'll pick the apples, and you boys are going to help peel them," Mrs. Hatford replied. "Two bushels of apples would take me two days, but with six of us working, I figure we could do it in a couple of hours."

"Oh, Mom, not that!" Wally complained.

"You won't groan when you see my apple pies," his mother said, getting in the car. "Don't forget your sandwiches, now. They're on the counter." And the car backed down the drive.

Caroline watched as Jake, Josh, Wally, and Peter came out the back door and sat on the steps to eat their sandwiches. They talked about how far you could shoot with a BB gun, and which decayed first after you died, your teeth or your bones.

They were too far away for Caroline to catch every word, but she wished the boys would tell a story on Wally—something embarrassing he had done. She'd tell it around at school, and Wally would wonder how she knew.

When the boys had finished eating, Josh brought out a sketchbook of some kind, and seemed to be drawing funny pictures in it, because the boys were all laughing.

"That's her, all right!" she heard Wally hoot. "That's just how she looked up there onstage, holding her book out in front of her like that. Yeah, make the corners of her mouth turn down, Josh, like she's about to bawl."

Caroline's cheeks flamed a second time. Josh was drawing a picture of her! Wally must have told them all about listening to her up onstage.

"Write what she's saying, Josh," Wally continued. " 'Oh, come back, Ratty! Please, please do!' " He mimicked her in a high voice, and the boys howled, Peter loudest of all.

It was all Caroline could do to keep from bursting out of the toolshed right that minute and pounding Wally on the head. She wouldn't be surprised if he had told it at the dinner table in front of his parents. Now the boys were looking at other pictures in the sketchbook, and from their hoots and laughter, Caroline could tell that Josh had sketched other pictures of her and her sisters as well.

When the laughter died away at last, Wally came out into the yard with a small rubber ball and practiced catching by bouncing it against the shed.

Blang! Blang! Blang! Caroline's head began to pound. Each time the ball hit the metal shed it sounded like an explosion in a tin-can factory. On and on it went—at least twenty minutes. Caroline felt as though her head would split.

Finally Wally stopped, and all four boys lay down on their backs in the grass.

"What do you want to do?" Wally asked Josh.

"I don't know," said Josh. "What do you want to do?"

"Go to the school and shoot some baskets?" asked Jake.

"Naw," said Wally.

"Bug the girls?" asked Josh.

"Yeah!" said Peter, Jake, and Wally.

Ha! thought Caroline.

"We'd better wait awhile, they're probably having Sunday dinner," Josh told them.

"Man!" said Jake. "I've thought of all *kinds* of stuff we could do to them at Halloween!"

"Yeah?" Caroline heard Josh say. "Wait till it *snows*! Boy, will we ever get them then."

"You remember how we used to sneak out on New Year's Eve with the Bensons, and Bill would blow his cornet right under someone's window at midnight? Wouldn't old Caroline flip?" said Wally.

"What about firecrackers?" said Peter. "We could put firecrackers in tin cans and set them on the Malloys' porch."

"They haven't even seen Smuggler's Cove yet."

"We could throw Eddie's dumb cap down the old coal mine, see if she'd crawl in after it. Bet she would too," Jake said. "Remember when Tony Benson crawled in there and the rescue squad had to get him out?"

"Wait till we get to junior high school. There are about a hundred things you can do to a girl's locker. We could wait until Beth put her coat in some morning, and then fix it so she couldn't get the lock open." Josh's voice.

"Ha! Put *Caroline* in a locker and keep her there all weekend!"

More laughter.

Back in the toolshed Caroline smiled to herself. This was even better than she'd thought. Here she was, hearing all their plans! Wait till she told her sisters. They'd know everything the boys were going to do before they did it. No matter what the boys tried, the girls would be ready. This was far more fun than Ohio!

"Wait till the town picnic next summer. Man, we'll beat the girls at *every*thing," said Jake. "The relay race, the sack race, the three-legged race . . ."

". . . the skateboard contest . . ."

". . . the pie-eating contest . . ."

". . . volleyball."

There was a long silence then, and for a moment Caroline thought the boys might have gone inside. She put her eye to the crack again. They were still on the grass.

"Unless . . ." Wally said, and Jake finished for him.

". . . they go back to Ohio."

"Yeah," said Josh. "If the Bensons come back, it's over."

More silence.

"You know what I wish?" said Wally. "I hope the Bensons stay in Georgia long enough for us to do everything we've planned to do to the Malloys, and then come back."

"Yeah," said Jake. "That would be perfect."

"A year and a half, maybe," said Josh.

"Right," said Wally.

"Let's play horseshoes for a while," Jake suggested. He got to his feet and started straight toward the shed.

No! He was coming here! Caroline scrambled off

the toolbox, grabbing her lunch sack, and tried to hide behind the lawn mower.

The footsteps grew louder, then the sound of the hinges creaking as the door to the toolshed opened partway. Caroline saw Jake's hand reach inside for the horseshoes on one shelf. She flattened herself against the back wall, but it was no use. Jake saw.

"What . . . ?" His eyes opened wide. "Hey, guys, look what we caught!" Jake grinned as he opened the door wider. The others came running.

"It's Caroline!" said Peter.

"Spying on us!" cried Wally.

And before Caroline could scramble back over the lawn mower and make her escape, Jake slammed the door shut.

"Bring me the bicycle padlock, Wally!" he yelled. "We've got a hostage, and her sisters aren't getting her back without a ransom!"

Kidnapped!

Fourteen

Hornswoggled

Wally and his brothers could not believe their good fortune! Caroline Malloy, trapped in the tool-shed, and their parents away picking apples.

"We got her! We got her!" Peter sang, dancing around the yard. And then he stopped. "What's a hostage, Wally?"

"A person you keep prisoner until somebody pays to get her back," Wally told him. But then the enormity of what had happened began to sink in on him. How could this be? Only a few minutes ago he and his brothers were lying on their backs talking about Halloween and New Year's, and suddenly Caroline Malloy was a prisoner in their toolshed!

"Man, they aren't going to believe what we're going to make them say to get her back, are they, Jake?" Josh was saying. "What was it they wanted us to promise to get our flashlight back?"

"I am honestly and truly sorry for the trouble I

have caused, and . . . something about an obedient servant of the realm," said Wally.

"They are going to *crawl*!" said Jake. "They are going to *creep*! They are going to *beg*! We're going to rub their noses in the dirt before we give their sister back. You hear that, Caroline?" he yelled.

There was no answer from the toolshed.

"Probably crying," said Peter. He looked around a little worriedly.

"You crying, Caroline?" asked Josh.

"Hoo boy, can she cry! You ought to see her up there onstage! The tears just pour," Wally put in.

"Well, we didn't make her go in the shed," said Josh.

"Right!" said Peter. "She went in there all by herself, didn't she, Wally?"

"How are we going to get a note to her sisters, though, without her parents finding out?" Wally wondered. "What if her folks start looking for her?"

"Then we've got to reach Beth and Eddie before they do. We'll say something about how we found her on our property," Jake decided.

"Yeah! Trespassing!" said Wally. "That's a crime, isn't it?"

"We could call the police!" Peter whooped.

"Her sisters will come and get her, you'll see," said Jake. "Come on. Let's write the note."

The boys went over to the back steps and sat down. Wally got a pencil and paper, and Jake dictated: " 'To whom it may concern . . .' "

" 'Namely, Whomper and Weirdo,' " added Josh.

" '. . . Caroline the Crazie was found spying on our property, and is now being held prisoner in our toolshed.' "

Wally wrote it down.

" 'If you tell anybody,' " Jake continued, " 'we will tell your folks all the stuff you've done so far to us. If you want to see Caroline again, you've got to crawl over to our house on your hands and knees . . .' "

" 'Lick our shoes . . .' " said Josh.

"They'll never do that," said Wally, "not even for Caroline."

"Okay. 'Crawl over to our house on your hands and knees and say, *We are honestly and truly sorry for the trouble we have caused, and . . .*' " Jake paused again.

" '*Will be your obedient servants. . . .*' " said Josh.

"No. Obedient slaves," said Jake. "That's it. '*We are honestly and truly sorry for the trouble we have caused, and will be your obedient slaves forever.*' "

"Perfect," said Josh.

Wally started to write it, then stopped. "I can't imagine Eddie saying 'your obedient slave forever.' "

"Yeah," said Josh gloomily. "I can't imagine them crawling on their hands and knees either."

"Well, they thought *we* would say something

like this!" Jake reminded him. "Go ahead. Write it, Wally. Make them squirm a little. Maybe they *won't* do any of it, but they've got to at least say they're sorry."

Wally finished the note.

"How do we sign it?" Josh wondered.

"How did they sign theirs?" asked Jake.

"The Malloy Musketeers," said Wally.

Jake thought a minute. "The Hatford Hooligans," he decided, and they all signed their names.

"Who's going to deliver it?" asked Josh. "Peter?"

"Are you crazy?" said Jake. "They'll simply kidnap Peter!"

"We'll *all* deliver it!" said Josh. "All four of us will go over there together. Caroline can't escape, don't worry."

The boys looked toward the toolshed again.

"Hey, Caroline!" Wally called.

No answer.

"Hey, Crazie!" called Josh.

Still no answer.

"Maybe she dug her way out," said Peter.

The boys started across the lawn. Wally was feeling a little uneasy. The sun was shining right on the metal shed, and he knew how hot it got in the summertime. It wasn't summer any longer, but it was still warm. Maybe she had overheated. Maybe she was dead!

"Listen, guys, I don't know if we ought to keep

her in there," he said. "That shed gets awfully hot in the afternoons."

"Did *we* put her there?" Jake said. "It was her idea. She would have stayed all day, I'll bet, if we hadn't found her. All we did was put a padlock on the door."

"But suppose she got sick or something?" Wally said. "Man, we'd really catch it."

They stopped outside the shed.

"Hey, Caroline," Josh said again. "Are you dead?"

"Oh, she's just playing possum to make you open the door," said Jake.

"Remember that hot day in August when our old dog got distemper?" Wally reminded them. They looked at each other uneasily.

"Hey, Caroline, you want some water?" Wally called.

No answer. No sound at all.

Jake dialed the combination on the lock and opened the door, just a little.

They all stepped backward. Caroline was sitting on the floor of the shed, her eyes closed. White foam was oozing out one corner of her mouth.

"What's the matter with her?" asked Peter.

"I don't know," said Jake. "Hey, Caroline, come on out. You can go home now."

Caroline opened her eyes once, and they looked wild. Then they closed again.

"Jake . . . !" Wally said worriedly.

"Go on home, Caroline," Jake said.

The girl didn't move.

"What are we going to do?" asked Wally, and his heart began to pound.

"Forget the note," said Jake, and Wally knew he was worried too. "Go call her sisters, Wally, and tell them to come and get her. That Caroline's over here sick."

Wally made a beeline for the house, and went up the steps two at a time.

He quickly dialed the Malloys' number. What if the parents answered? What was he supposed to say? That Caroline was locked in the toolshed foaming at the mouth?

The phone rang five times before anyone answered.

"Hello?" It sounded like Eddie.

"Your sister's sick," said Wally.

There was a pause. "Who is this?" Eddie asked.

"Wally. Caroline's in our toolshed. You better come and get her."

"Yeah? What kind of a trick is this?" Eddie said. "I saw your folks drive away. You must think we're really stupid."

Wally's hand felt sweaty on the telephone. "Listen," he said again. "I mean it. She's foaming at the mouth."

"What?"

"We just unlocked the shed and I think she's got distemper. There's white stuff all over her lips."

"Hold on." It sounded as though Eddie had her hand over the receiver and was talking to somebody else. Then Beth came on the line.

"What's the matter with Caroline?" Beth asked.

"I already said! She's foaming at the mouth and acting weird, and you better come get her."

"How did she get in your shed?" asked Beth.

"She went there herself. We didn't put her there. She was spying on us."

"Then how did the shed get locked?"

"After we found her, we locked the door."

"Well, if you locked her in there and she's sick, you better call an ambulance," Beth said, and hung up.

Wally stared at the phone in his hand. Then slowly replaced the receiver and went out to the others on the back steps.

"Are they coming?" asked Jake.

Wally shook his head. "They said to call an ambulance."

"Hoo boy!" Josh whistled through his teeth. "We can't call an ambulance! Dad would be furious!"

"Yeah, but if something happened to her and we didn't, he'd kill us," Wally said.

The boys stared at each other. "You think we should try to carry her home ourselves?" Jake said.

"Let's try," said Wally.

They went back to the shed again. Caroline had

crawled behind the lawn mower now, and was making strange noises, half dog, half human.

"What's she doing?" asked Peter, eyes wide.

"Biting her own arm!" breathed Josh, and the boys retreated slowly to the back steps.

"What if she's rabid?" asked Wally.

"Don't be dumb."

"What if she *is*? What if a strange dog bit her before they left Ohio and nobody even knew it?"

Jake let out his breath. "Boy, I hope she leaves before Mom and Dad get home." He hunched his shoulders. "Look," he said to Wally. "Go call Beth and Eddie again, and tell them we'll make a deal. They come and get Caroline, and we'll call off the war for good. No more tricks again ever."

Wally went back inside and called the Malloys. Eddie answered again.

"Listen," he began. It was all he could think of to say. "Come over and get Caroline, and we'll call off the war for good. No more tricks again ever."

"No deal," Eddie said, and the receiver clicked again.

Wally reported it to the others.

"They *have* to take her!" bleated Jake. "She's their *sister*! What kind of sisters are they if they won't even come and get someone who's rabid!"

"What time is it?" asked Josh.

Jake looked at his watch. "Almost two. Mom and Dad could be driving back any minute."

Wally's stomach seemed to turn upside down.

"It doesn't matter whether we took the padlock off or not," he said finally. "The fact is we *did* have the padlock on for a while, so that she couldn't get out if she'd wanted to. And she *was* in there for at least an hour. That might have been long enough to do it. We're responsible no matter what."

"I'm not touching her," said Josh.

"Me either," said Peter.

"*I'll* call the Malloys," Jake said, and his voice sounded a little shaky. Wally went back inside with him. Jake dialed.

This time the phone must have rung ten times before Eddie answered.

"Yes?" she said loudly, impatiently. Wally was standing three feet away and he could hear every word she said. "What is it *now*?"

"Look," Jake began.

"Look . . . listen. . . . Is that all you guys can say?"

"We'll make any kind of deal you want if you just come and get Caroline," Jake told her.

The silence this time must have lasted for ten whole seconds. To Wally it seemed forever.

"Any kind of deal we want?"

"Yeah. Just come and get her."

"Say, 'Please.' "

"Please," murmured Jake.

"Say, 'Pretty please.' "

Wally heard Jake swallow. "Pretty please," he said.

"Say, 'Pretty please from your faithful and obedient servant.' "

"Hey, listen. . . ."

"*Say* it!"

"Pretty please from your . . ."

There was the sound of a car pulling in the drive.

"The *folks* are home!" Jake said into the receiver. "Come and get her! Hurry!"

"Say the rest. . . ."

"Your faithful, obedient servant," Jake said, and hung up the phone. "I think I'm going to throw up," he said to Wally.

Fifteen

Bamboozled

Caroline was beginning to wonder how much longer she had to roll around the floor of the shed with marshmallow on her lips before her sisters came after her.

It was entirely by accident that she had discovered the marshmallow foam. Once she found that the boys had padlocked the door, she had popped a marshmallow into her mouth for energy, then realized how thirsty she was. Sloshing the marshmallow sauce around in her mouth, she was thinking that if she ever had to play the part of a madwoman, she could use marshmallow foam. And it didn't take long to decide what to do when the boys came again to check on her. All she had to do to make *that* happen was be quiet.

Little snatches of conversation came from the steps across the yard. "They *have* to take her. . . ." "I'm not touching her. . . ." "We're responsible. . . ." Caroline decided that if she didn't need a drink of water so much, she could probably hold out for another couple of hours.

The next thing she heard was the sound of a car pulling in the drive, but even before it stopped, the back door slammed and she heard Jake say quickly, "They're coming! Beth and Eddie are on the way."

What should she do now, she wondered. This could be her grandest performance yet. Should she go on pretending to be rabid, so that Beth and Eddie had to carry her home? Or should she wait until her sisters opened the door of the shed, and then they could all have a big laugh together? Or maybe she could make a grand entrance now, by herself, and—

"*Three* bushels of apples," she heard Mrs. Hatford saying. "They were the best I've seen in a long, long time. And I don't want to hear any complaining. You didn't want to help pick them, so you can certainly help peel them. Won't do you one bit of harm."

She had better wait until the parents had gone inside, Caroline thought. Mrs. Hatford might figure out right away what was on her lips, and she didn't want to reveal the joke until Beth and Eddie were there.

The back door slammed as Mr. and Mrs. Hatford went inside. Three minutes later there came the crunch of footsteps on the gravel drive, and the sound of girls' low voices. Caroline could hardly keep from laughing out loud, and when Eddie opened the door of the shed at last, Caroline was sitting on the floor grinning, a marshmallow perched on her head.

The three burst out laughing.

"I *told* you it was probably marshmallow," said Beth. "I *knew* she couldn't get that sick in two hours."

"Oh, Eddie," Caroline shrieked happily. "It was my best performance. They thought I was rabid! They thought I was mad! They were even afraid to touch me."

"Did you know they called three times trying to get us to come and get you?" Beth giggled.

"And you know what we made them say?" asked Eddie. "Your faithful, obedient servant."

The girls howled.

They turned and started back across the yard. Josh and Jake were still on the steps with Peter, their faces pink with embarrassment.

Just then the back door opened and out stepped Mrs. Hatford, carrying a huge pan of apples. Mr. Hatford was behind her, carrying one of the bushels.

"Hello, girls," she called cheerfully.

Caroline, Beth, and Eddie stopped dead in their tracks.

"Wally just told me you were coming," Mrs. Hatford went on. "How nice of you to volunteer! I think we could do them right here in the yard, don't you?"

The girls stared in astonishment, then gave a low moan as Wally, paring knives in hand, came down the back steps with a smile wide as Christmas.

THE GIRLS GET EVEN

Phyllis Reynolds Naylor

A YEARLING BOOK

To the students of East Main Street School and Buckhannon-Upshur Intermediate School in Buckhannon, West Virginia, which is almost, but not quite, where this story takes place.

Published by
Bantam Doubleday Dell Books for Young Readers
a division of
Bantam Doubleday Dell Publishing Group, Inc.
1540 Broadway
New York, New York 10036

ISBN: 0-440-40971-3

Reprinted by arrangement with Delacorte Press

Printed in the United States of America

July 1994

10 9 8 7 6 5 4 3

OPM

Contents

• • • • •

One

Making Plans

"Wait till Halloween!"

That was the battle cry these days, except that neither Caroline nor her sisters were sure exactly how Halloween would change things. No matter what they thought of to get even, there were always tricks the boys might play on them that would be far worse.

Caroline could not get it out of her mind. Her fingers were still sore from peeling all those apples for Mrs. Hatford, because Mrs. Hatford thought that's what Caroline had come over to do. And if Caroline had told her that the boys had locked her in their shed, she would have had to explain why she'd been over there spying on them in the first place.

And if she'd said she'd been trying to catch Wally Hatford doing something embarrassing so she could humiliate him the way he had humiliated her, she would have had to explain what had happened before that, and then before that, all the way back to when the Malloys had moved to Buckman in August and the Hatford boys had tried to drive them out. It was just too complicated, and neither her parents nor the boys' parents would stand for such nonsense one moment if they knew.

What their parents didn't understand was that Caroline and her sisters could no more go without getting even than they could go without breathing. In fact, half the fun of getting even was to see what the boys would think up next, just so Caroline, Beth, and Eddie could "get even" all over again. They'd never had so much excitement back in Ohio.

"You know," Mother said at breakfast that Saturday, "I'm beginning to love living in a big old house like this. If we move back to Ohio, Ralph, I think we should build an addition onto that house."

"We'll see," Coach Malloy murmured, munching his toast over NFL ratings in the paper.

Caroline exchanged helpless looks with her two older sisters. *If we move back to Ohio . . . ?* There was still the possibility that Dad would go back to his old coaching job there? As much as Caroline had hated the thought of moving to West

Virginia in the first place, she now desperately wished to stay.

Where else would they find a group of ready-made rivals just their ages? Where else would they live on a road called Island Avenue? The large piece of land in the middle of Buckman was not really an island, because it was surrounded on only three sides by water, but people called their road "Island Avenue" anyway. If you were coming into town on Island Avenue, you kept going until you were out on the very tip, and then you crossed the bridge over into the business district. You might not even have noticed that the river on your right was the same river that was on your left; it simply looped about at the end of the island.

This little college town had everything that their home back in Ohio did not—even a swinging footbridge across the river connecting them to the college campus and the street that led to the school. Caroline, who was only eight but was in fourth grade because she was precocious, dreamed of being an actress someday. And when she saw the river, the footbridge, the large old house they would live in, and the old school with a real stage and velvet curtain, she knew that this was the place she would make her debut.

•

Caroline was standing in front of the mirror in her room, her long thick ponytail tucked up under one of her mother's hats—the navy-blue hat with a veil that Mother reserved for funerals. She was pretending to be the wife of a captain who had been drowned at sea. She was practicing going from sad to grief-stricken to hysterical when she heard Eddie, the oldest, clattering up the stairs.

Caroline stopped being grief-stricken and ran to the door of her room.

"News!" Eddie yelped, taking off the baseball cap she wore always and tossing it into the air. "Have I got news!"

Beth stepped out of the bathroom, toothbrush still in her mouth. A year younger than Eddie, ten-year-old Beth had the most beautiful teeth in the Malloy family because she brushed them longer than anyone else. And the reason she brushed them longer was because she always read while she brushed and got so absorbed in her book that she just stood there, going over and over the same teeth for three, four, or even five minutes at a time, her mind on *The Zombie's Revenge* or something.

"Caroline, take off that stupid hat," Eddie said. "We're going camping."

The hat came off with a yank. *"What?"*

"I was in the hardware store buying a wrench for my bike when I heard Mrs. Hatford tell a customer that her boys were going camping tonight at Smuggler's Cove."

"Ohhhh!" The very name was delicious. *Smuggler's Cove.* Caroline could almost see people moving about in the moonlight, silent figures carrying sacks off boats and hiding them in caves. The wonderful thing about being an actress, or even *wanting* to be an actress, is that she saw everything as a story, and herself in the starring role.

"But we weren't invited!" said Beth, the toothpaste still foamy around her mouth.

"Of *course* we weren't invited. That's why we're going." Eddie (who was really Edith Ann, but hated her name) picked up her cap from the floor and placed it on her head again, backwards.

"It's a wonderful idea!" cried Caroline. "It's been warm all day. A *perfect* day for camping!"

"We don't even know where Smuggler's Cove is," Beth protested.

"We're going to follow the boys," Eddie said, "only they don't know it. We've got to stay just far enough behind them that they don't see us."

"Then what?" Caroline asked excitedly, her dark eyes shining.

Eddie leaned forward, one arm around Caroline's shoulders, the other around Beth's. *"Then,"* she said, "we steal out in the night and take their clothes."

Both Caroline and Beth shrieked delightedly. Beth was fair-haired and pale-skinned and tended to list to one side in a strong wind. There was no wind here in the upstairs hallway of the house the Malloys were renting, but excitement did the same thing to Beth, and it was only because Eddie had an arm around her that she didn't collapse on the spot.

"They'll have to come back home in their PJs!" Beth cried happily.

"What if they don't wear pajamas?" Caroline asked.

"Then they'll have to come home in their underwear," said Eddie.

"What if they don't sleep in their underwear?" Caroline asked mischievously.

"Then they'll have to walk home stark naked!" said Eddie, and the girls whooped.

•

"We're going camping," Eddie said as the three girls surrounded their mother in the kitchen. "Could we pack our dinner—something to eat cold without cooking?"

Mrs. Malloy looked up from the coupons she was sorting on the table. "Overnight? Where are you going?"

"Smuggler's Cove," Caroline said.

"What?"

"It's a favorite camping spot," Father called from the next room. "I've heard students talk about it on campus."

"Well, I don't know. . . ." said Mother. "I'm not sure—"

"Oh, Jean, don't baby them," Coach Malloy said. "I think it's fine that they want to go camping. Get out in the fresh air and sunshine. Let them go."

Mother sighed. "We don't even have a tent."

"We don't need one! We'll sleep under the stars," Eddie told her. "It's gorgeous out."

So while Mother planned their dinner, the girls ran upstairs for their sleeping bags.

"I heard Mrs. Hatford telling this woman in the hardware store that the boys were going as soon as Jake and Josh finish their paper route this afternoon," Eddie said. "What we've got to do is sit up here with the binoculars. As soon as they start out, we'll follow, just far enough behind that we don't lose them."

Caroline could already see herself as the scout, the spy, Agent XOX, crawling over the desert sand on her stomach, braving the dangers of the night as she slipped one hand under the tent flap and made off with the boys' clothes.

She should really be wearing a cape, she decided—a long black cape with a hood that partially covered her face. But there weren't any capes in the Malloy household, so she settled for a large orange poncho that her father wore for college football games when it rained.

She put it on and it dragged the floor. She held it close beneath her chin and watched herself sideways in the mirror as she moved silently around the room.

"Caroline, cut the comedy!" Eddie scolded from the doorway. "The boys could be leaving any minute, and we've got to be ready."

Caroline took off the poncho as Eddie turned on Beth next: "Why are you taking two books? There's not going to be any time to read."

"Just in case," Beth told her. "What do you care, Eddie? I'm the one who's carrying them."

Eddie rolled her eyes and went downstairs to get their dinner.

When Caroline was packed, a sweater, poncho, and pajamas inside her bedroll, she crouched down at her window with Father's binoculars and watched the house across the river with its little balcony on top—a "widow's walk," it was called—supposedly for the wives of sea captains so each could watch for her husband's ship on the horizon. There wasn't any sea near West Virginia, of course—just the shiny horseshoe of a river curving around the end of Island Avenue.

Caroline could make out the two younger boys, Wally and Peter, sitting on the steps, their camping gear behind them, waiting for Jake and Josh to get home. Wally was nine and in the same grade as Caroline. Peter was only seven, and if he hadn't been a Hatford, Caroline thought, she might have liked him because he was sweet and innocent, going along with whatever his brothers thought up because he didn't know any better.

It was Jake and Josh, the eleven-year-old twins, she suspected, who had made the plans about driving the Malloys from Buckman. Jake, especially, who seemed to be the ringleader. But in some ways Josh was worse, because he kept a sketchpad of drawings that made his brothers laugh, and Caroline knew that most of those drawings were cartoons of her and her sisters. When she saw the twins returning with their canvas carriers slung over their shoulders, she gave the signal to Beth, who gave the signal to Eddie, and in minutes the girls were crossing the swinging bridge single file.

They cut through the yard between the Hatfords' place and a neighbor's, careful to stay behind bushes all the way.

Finally they heard the back door slam, and the

four Hatford boys came down the steps, went out the gate at the back of their property, and headed for the woods on the edge of town. Somewhere, in those woods or beyond, was Smuggler's Cove.

Two

Smuggler's Cove

It seemed to Wally, sitting on the steps beside Peter, that what he was looking at right now was life. He was studying an anthill built over a crack in the sidewalk. The way the ants were struggling and pushing, each trying to get to the top of the anthill first, reminded him of the way the Hatfords and Malloys had been quarreling since August. As though their quarrel was the most important thing in the world.

"You know what?" he said to Peter. "The ants don't even know we're here. Look." He put his sneakered foot in the path of a large ant hurrying toward the anthill, and it just scurried on around the toe. Didn't even look up to see what giant was blocking its path. Didn't even know that the toe was attached to a foot, and the foot to a leg, and the leg to a body.

"Maybe it's nice to be an ant," he added. "Someone could come along any minute and smash the anthill and they don't even know it. They don't even worry, because it never even crosses their minds."

Peter got up and brought his foot down on the anthill.

Wally stared. "Why did you do *that*?"

"You *said*!"

"I didn't tell you to step on it! You've killed them!"

Peter looked around. "There's more," he said defensively, and sat back down.

Wally sighed. He couldn't help looking up at the sky just then, in case there was the slightest chance of a monstrous foot hanging over him and Peter. He wished that Jake and Josh would hurry and get home from their paper route. On a warm October Saturday like this the battle with the Malloy girls seemed about as important as which ant got to the anthill first. And he, for one, was going to enjoy camping with his brothers—just four guys out in the woods by themselves.

As much as he tried to forget them, however, his mind ran through the inventory of grievances against the girls: the way they had climbed onto the Hatfords' roof one night when Mom and Dad were away and howled through the trapdoor; the way they had spied on the boys from the shed, tricked them into washing the Malloys' windows, and thrown Mom's chocolate chiffon cake in the river.

Wally was smiling in spite of himself. Watching Caroline's face after she'd realized it *was* a cake was the most fun of all. Then he blinked. *Fun?* Did he think *fun*? Was it possible that despite all his grumbling, he *liked* having the girls around?

"What are you grinning about?" asked Peter.

"I was thinking of chocolate cake," Wally told him.

•

"Ham sandwiches, potato salad, Oreo cookies, and apples," said Mother, handing a large bag to Josh as the boys strapped on their gear in the kitchen. "Plus orange drink and doughnuts for breakfast."

"I'll carry the doughnuts," Peter volunteered.

"No, you won't," Jake told him. "The last time you carried the food, you ate all around the edge of two doughnuts. Who's got the water?"

"I have," said Wally.

"Tent?"

"Check," said Josh.

"Flashlight?"

"Check," said Wally.

"I've got the corn chips!" Peter told them.

They were off. Not only did they not have to brush after eating, Wally thought as he went out the back gate with his brothers and headed down the alley, but they could stay up as late as they wanted, and miss Sunday school tomorrow as well.

The bedroll was snug and warm against his back, the leaves thick on the ground, and Wally decided he had never seen such a beautiful October as this one. He could hear the marching band on the college campus, practicing for the homecoming parade the following weekend. Overhead a hawk soared lazily, its wings not even moving. This was a time for eating your supper on a log, lying on your back under the stars, and dreaming about what you were going to be on Halloween.

His left sneaker was sliding up and down on his heel, and Wally looked down to see his shoelace flopping about. He stopped and bent over to tie it, and then his eyes grew large. Staring backwards between his legs he saw, or thought he saw, three figures with packs on their backs who looked all too familiar.

As he stared, however, the three figures seemed to disappear into the trees on either side. Wally stood up and took a deep breath. And then, without even turning around, he caught up with Jake and Josh and Peter.

"Don't anybody look now—don't stop or turn or anything—but we're being followed," he said.

Peter's eyes were like two fried eggs, and his back got as stiff as a broom. "Who is it?"

"Who's the worst you can think of?" Wally said in answer.

"A gorilla?" Peter gulped.

"A motorcycle gang," said Josh. "With chains wrapped around their fists."

But Jake's face registered horror. *"Them?"* he whispered.

"Them," said Wally. "But don't look. They don't know that we know."

"Who?" Peter demanded.

"Peter, don't you turn around one second. Don't even glance back there, or you're dead meat. Understand?" Jake warned him.

"Who *is* it?" Peter cried. "Robbers?"

"A whomper, a weirdo, and a crazie," Wally answered, reciting the nicknames they'd given Eddie, Beth, and Caroline—Eddie, for the way she could hit a ball; Beth, for the kind of books she read; and Caroline, for turning everything that ever happened to her into a movie.

"Oh, them!" said Peter, obviously relieved. "Are they coming with us?"

"No, they're not coming with us!" croaked Jake.

The boys tramped on, not daring to look around. "Well, I don't know, Jake. I think they're coming whether we want them to or not," Wally said. "They have packs on their backs."

Josh let out his breath. "Somebody must have told them we were going camping. What are we going to do, Jake?"

"Do?" his twin replied. "We are going to make them sorry they tagged along."

"Can I turn around yet?" asked Peter.

"No!" Jake said. "Don't even move your head." And then to Wally, "Think! What would be the worst thing that could happen to them?"

Wally tried to think of the worst thing that had ever happened to *him* in the woods. "Get lost," he said.

Jake's face lit up. "That's *it*! It'll be almost dark in an hour or so. We'll lead the girls every which way until they don't know which end is up. Then we'll sneak down to Smuggler's Cove and have it all to ourselves."

"Wow!" said Peter, his head never moving an inch.

•

It was when they were crossing the creek for the third time that Wally realized they could have been at camp long ago, enjoying their ham sandwiches, if they hadn't felt obliged to lose the girls.

Every so often he or his brothers would slip off into the bushes and wait just long enough to see the girls trailing far behind, and then the boys were off again, hoping to get them royally lost before dark closed in completely.

It was chilly now that the sun was down, and Wally began to wish he had brought his ski cap, as Mom had suggested. Fires were forbidden in the woods in the fall, but once they put up the tent and crawled inside their sleeping bags, they'd be okay.

Wait a minute, he thought. They'd come all the way out here just so he could go to bed at seven o'clock? If he was home he could be watching TV until eleven!

"We've lost them good!" Jake whispered, coming through the bushes behind them. "They're so far back, they'll never catch up. Let's go to the cove and set up camp."

Eager for dinner, the boys hurried through the trees in the direction of the river, and even though Wally's foot slipped once or twice in the mud along the bank, he didn't complain. The last quarter mile or so he turned on the flashlight to see where they were going, and at last they reached the rocky inlet circled by pine trees where the Hatford and Benson boys used to camp summer after summer. Here the river lapped gently against the bank, and the crevasses between the rocks looked deep and forbidding in the near darkness.

"I'll bet old Caroline's bawling her eyes out right now," said Josh.

"How are they going to find their way home?" Peter wanted to know. He was holding the flashlight while his brothers set up the tent. Every so often he tired of holding it still and scanned the trees with it instead, and then all three boys yelled together: "Peter!"

"How are they going to get home?" he asked again.

"That's their problem," said Jake.

"What are they going to eat?" asked Peter, sounding worried.

"That's their problem too," Jake answered. "Did we ask them to follow us out here? Not on your life."

Inside the tent it wasn't so bad. Not so cold, at least. Just crowded. Four boys in one pup tent was two boys too many, but at least it was warmer that way.

Wally didn't think he had ever tasted better ham sandwiches in his life. Thin-sliced ham, with yellow mustard on thick slabs of homemade bread.

Big juicy apples. One carton of potato salad with onion and peppers, and a whole box of Oreo cookies to divide among them, not to mention the doughnuts and orange drink for breakfast.

They all felt much better after they had eaten.

"This is the life!" said Jake, stretching out as best he could on his sleeping bag. "Remember the year the Bensons brought their fishing poles and we had fish for dinner?"

"And the time a mole dug right up into the tent?" said Wally. "And the way Bill Benson used to imitate an owl, and Peter got scared?"

"I did not!" Peter declared. "I knew it was Bill all the time."

"I wonder if they'll ever move back," Wally said, thinking of Bill, Danny, Steve, Tony, and Doug down in Georgia, having a "Georgia peach" for a teacher, and a whole new state to explore. What if their father decided he liked teaching in Atlanta and wanted to stay? What if the Malloys decided they liked being in the Bensons' old house and bought it from them?

It took a lot of fixing and rearranging to get all the sleeping bags squeezed into the pup tent. Everyone complained when Wally took off the sneaker that had got wet and muddy, so he put it back on again, right over his smelly sock.

When they were settled down at last, Wally

turned off the flashlight, and put his hands under his head, staring up into the darkness of the tent. He was wedged between Peter and the left side of the tent, but he was warm at last—and feeling really good with seven Oreo cookies in his stomach.

What did people do who had no brothers? What if he had been born into a family of girls? Three *Malloy* girls! It was a thought too awful to think.

Jake and Josh were trying to make up another verse to "Ninety-nine Bottles of Beer on the Wall," once you got down to "one bottle of beer on the wall," but after a while Jake's voice faded out, then Josh's. Peter had long since fallen asleep, one arm slung over Wally's chest. Finally even Josh stopped singing, and then it was just the sounds of the woods at night—rustling in the bushes, the shrill call of a night bird, the wind blowing through the branches overhead, a deep snore from Josh. . . .

Wally played around with the flashlight awhile, making circles of light on the ceiling of the tent; practiced making distress signals, dots and dashes, with the light. But his eyes began to close, his fingers lost their grip, and finally he tucked the flashlight behind his head and settled down to sleep.

He didn't know when he awakened whether

he had been asleep only a few minutes or an hour, but he felt something moving along his side.

He lay still as a stone. A snake? A *poisonous* snake? Should he move? Should he very, very slowly sit up and wake the others?

Maybe it was another mole. A mouse, perhaps. A harmless little field mouse.

Carefully, carefully, trying not to move his body at all, Wally reached back behind his head for the flashlight. Slowly raising his head so that he could see, he aimed the flashlight toward the moving creature by his side and turned it on.

A hand. A human hand. Wally yelled bloody murder.

Three

The Bargain

Caroline was half convinced they would all three die in the woods, and their bodies would not be found until spring. Beth was so tired of going up and down hills and jumping across creeks and climbing over fallen trees that she seemed to be listing to one side rather dangerously. It was also growing dark sooner than they'd thought.

"I think we should all just lie down beside each other with our arms folded over our chests and die peacefully," Caroline said in a hoarse whisper, ever the actress.

"I think you've got rhubarb where your brains should be," Eddie scolded. "Quit whining, you two, and turn on the flashlight."

Beth got out the flashlight. It shone on the path ahead, but the trees still loomed up dark on either side.

"We could all write a farewell note to Mom and Dad, and tell them to give our possessions to the orphans," said Caroline, her voice trembling dramatically.

Eddie wheeled around. "Caroline, will you just shut up? You're not helping things a bit."

"Well, I don't see any point in going any farther when we don't know where we are," Beth said. "We lost the boys a half hour ago, so we might just as well camp here. It's almost dark, and we're starved."

"Listen!" Eddie said suddenly, and the girls stood still.

Caroline listened so hard, she felt her ears were growing, but all she could hear was her own pulse throbbing in her head. And then, far, far away, she thought she heard noises.

"Voices!" Beth confirmed. They listened some more.

"Are you sure they're *human* voices?" Caroline asked. "It could be animal voices. What do raccoons sound like?"

They remained very still and listened again, ears to the wind.

"It almost . . . sounds like singing," Beth said.

They waited.

"It *is* singing," Eddie declared. "It's—"

" 'Ninety-nine Bottles of Beer on the Wall,' " Caroline finished.

"The boys!" the three girls said together.

It took almost fifteen minutes more to get to the place where they could see the tent. First the singing seemed to be coming from one direction. Then the wind changed, and it came from another. Beth got her foot caught in a vine and they had to take her shoe off to get her foot loose. Then it took several more minutes to find the shoe.

By that time the singing had stopped altogether, but Caroline caught sight of a light, a little circle of light, and finally they could hear the river and make out the beam of a flashlight from inside a small tent.

"Bingo!" said Eddie softly. "Okay, let's make camp."

•

Lying on a bed of leaves in the daytime was a lot more pleasant than lying on a bed of leaves in the dark was going to be, with no tent over them, Caroline decided.

As the girls spread out their sleeping bags beneath the trees, Caroline wondered about wild animals.

"Are there bears in West Virginia?" she whispered.

"Cut it out, Caroline," said Eddie.

But Beth gave a little gasp. "Are there?"

"If there are bears in West Virginia, they're way up in the mountains," Eddie said.

Caroline knew that Eddie didn't know what she was talking about any more than Beth knew about bears, but she didn't ask any other questions because she didn't really want to know the answers. She unzipped her sleeping bag, took off her shoes, and crawled in.

"Who's going to steal their clothes?" Beth whispered.

"I am, as soon as I'm sure they're asleep," said Eddie.

Caroline scrunched down as far as she could into her sleeping bag, feeling secure with Eddie on one side of her and Beth on the other. Within minutes Beth began her noisy sleep that sounded like a motorcycle revving up. And then, Caroline could tell from Eddie's slow measured breathing next to her that she had fallen asleep as well.

How could this be? Caroline lay with her eyes wide open. They had come all this way to steal the boys' clothes, and Eddie was asleep? She was just about to poke her and remind her of her obligations, when she remembered the poncho she'd brought along, and Agent XOX. Wasn't it she herself who should be the spy, the scout, the secret agent—creeping through the trees, slithering along the ground, and stealing the boys' clothes?

"Caroline did it again!" her sisters would say in awe.

Wriggling back out of the sleeping bag, she put on her sneakers and picked up the flashlight. Caroline pulled the rubberized poncho over her and then, like a small tepee moving along the ground, set out softly for the boys' tent.

The boys, she figured, would have taken off their clothes and thrown them at the foot of their sleeping bags or perhaps wadded them down between their sleeping bags and the sides of the tent. If she could just slip her hand underneath, perhaps she could pull the clothes out from under the edge without having to open the tent flap at all. Unless, of course, the tent had a canvas floor.

She turned off the flashlight when she reached the tent. Like fingers searching out the keys on a piano, Caroline's fingers inched their way beneath one side. She was in luck. No floor. She lay down on her stomach and extended her arm, her fingers exploring inside the tent.

There was something there, all right. A down jacket? Or was it a sleeping bag she was feeling? She couldn't see a thing, of course, because the poncho had slipped down over her face. Now her hand touched something else and her fingers ran along the edge. Something warm. Somebody's pajamas?

"Yipes!" There was a yell from inside the tent.

She tried to pull her hand back, but someone had grabbed it.

Another yell. A bleat. A bellow. "A hand! Josh! Jake!"

Caroline rolled over, struggling hard to pull her arm loose, but someone was pressing it to the ground.

Pushing the poncho off her face, Caroline could see the beam of a flashlight inside the tent, see the jiggling of the canvas as the boys tumbled around, and then the tent flap opened and out they spilled.

"It's Caroline!" yelled Josh. "They found us!"

They found us? They knew? Whoever was inside the tent holding her arm let loose to come outside, and as soon as she was free, Caroline struggled to her feet but tripped on the long poncho and fell on her face again. The boys laughed and yelled.

More footsteps. Running footsteps. Caroline could hear Eddie's voice, trailed by Beth's. Somebody had hold of her feet and was pulling her toward the river. Was Agent XOX to die a drowning death?

"You let go of her!" came Eddie's voice, and suddenly Eddie had one arm, Beth the other, and they were pulling her the other way. Back and forth, back and forth. Secret Agent XOX was going to die a stretching death instead. Torn limb from limb.

"Keep hanging on, and we'll throw you all in!" Jake yelled to Caroline's sisters.

And then Peter's voice wailed sleepily from the door of the tent: "Wally, come back in! It's freezing!"

In that instant Eddie and Beth yanked Caroline free, and finally Caroline was on her feet again, half running, half stumbling back into the underbrush beside her sisters.

•

They sat on top of their sleeping bags while the boys whooped some more and shone the flashlight on them.

"They don't even have a tent!" exclaimed Peter.

"Hey, you girls lost?" Jake's voice.

"You cold? What were you looking for? A blanket?" Wally's.

"You want any directions, just ask us," called Josh. "We'll direct you right into the river."

"Yeah, who asked you to come on this camping trip?" called Jake.

It seemed just too much for Eddie. "You don't

own these woods! You don't own the river! We have as much right to be here as you do!" she screamed.

"Ha! You wouldn't even have found your way out here if you hadn't followed us!" Josh yelled.

"We saw you sneaking along, hiding behind bushes! We knew you were behind us all the time!" called Wally.

Caroline felt her face burning. How embarrassing to know that the boys had known they were back there all the time.

Josh and Jake were laughing again, shining the flashlight right in her eyes. "Old Caroline sneaking over here in that poncho. You look like a witch, Caroline!"

"They're all witches!" declared Josh. "They don't even need to dress up for Halloween. Just come as they are and they'll scare the little kids."

The boys laughed some more.

"Hey, girls!" came Jake's voice. "What are you going to be in the Halloween parade?"

"What Halloween parade?" Caroline called back, in spite of herself. If there was any dressing up in costumes to be done, she wanted to know about it.

"The school parade," yelled Wally. "We and the Bensons won first prize almost every year."

"Well, whatever we think of, it'll be a lot better than what *you* wear," Beth retorted.

"You wish!" said Josh.

"We'll win again, won't we, Wally?" came Peter's voice.

"Sure we will."

"Wanna bet?" yelled Eddie. "You must feel you own this town. You must think you're going to go on winning the prizes and hogging the best camping spots just because you lived here first. Well, I'll tell you something, wise guys. Maybe you *won't*! Maybe somebody else will win this year."

"Keep dreaming!" called Josh.

Caroline was beginning to shiver. The air seemed cooler than it had when she'd started out for the boys' tent, and she wished Beth and Eddie would crawl into their sleeping bags and shut up. But Eddie was angry, and when she was angry, she was unstoppable.

"Wanna bet?" she yelled again.

"Sure! Bet!" yelled Jake. "Whichever group wins first prize—you or us—will be the masters and the other group will be the slaves."

Were they crazy? Caroline wondered. *No one would agree to—*

"You're on!" Eddie yelled back. "Deal!"

Caroline gasped. "Eddie, are you nuts?"

"They think they're *so* smart!" Eddie sputtered. Caroline had never seen her so angry.

"What will the slaves have to do?" Caroline called out.

Josh answered, "Whatever the masters tell them to do."

There seemed to be a brief discussion going on in the boys' camp. Then Wally replied, "The slaves have to do all the masters' work for a whole month."

"Fine with us!" yelled Eddie.

"Eddie, if they win, they'll—" Beth began.

"They *won't*! *We* will!" Eddie said. And then, more desperately, "We *have* to!"

Caroline let out her breath. She was too tired to argue anymore. All she wanted was her warm sleeping bag and a soft place to lay her head. She had just started to crawl in when suddenly, *Splat.*

Caroline looked around. Another splat.

"Rain!" cried Beth and Eddie together.

The girls quickly rolled up their cotton sleeping bags, sat on top of them, and spread out the poncho over their heads, while the boys whooped again and tumbled back into their tent.

The rain came down harder and harder. Fifteen minutes. Twenty minutes. On and on. All around them the ground was getting soggy and spongy. A damp earth smell arose from the floor of the forest. Caroline felt like a mushroom. She smelled like a mushroom. She imagined that she had little bugs crawling up one side of her stalk and down the other.

The food was gone. The water was almost gone. Caroline needed to go to the bathroom, but she didn't want to get rained on, so she stayed where she was and felt miserable.

It was all such a dumb idea, following the boys out here to steal their clothes. They hadn't even taken their clothes off, come to think of it, and neither had she or her sisters.

"Hey, girls!" came a yell from down on the riverbank. "You going to stay there and get wet?"

"Why don't you find your way home?"

"Are your sleeping bags soggy?"

Caroline could hear her teeth chattering. Or maybe it was Eddie's or Beth's. For a while none of them moved. None of them spoke. The rain drummed on the poncho over their heads, and Caroline was sure that by morning it would have driven them all mad. None of them spoke; they were too disgusted and angry.

And then, after a long while, Eddie murmured, "Wait till Halloween!" And she said it with conviction.

Four

Spy

All the way home from Smuggler's Cove, Wally worried.

First, he worried that the girls might not have found their way home. When he and his brothers went looking for them the next morning, all they had found was a sock.

Second, he worried that if they *did* make it home all right, Caroline and her sisters really might win first prize in the Halloween parade, and he and his brothers would have to do the girls' work for a month. He tried to imagine going over to the Malloys' house for four Saturdays asking Caroline what needed doing. Imagined her telling him to make her bed and wash her clothes. Maybe even clean the toilets!

Josh must have been thinking the same thing. "Jake," he said as they turned up the alley behind their house, "maybe we should pull out of that bargain with the Malloys. What if we *don't* win?"

"We will!" Jake said. "Don't even talk about not winning! What we've got to do now is think up the best costumes we've ever had."

Wally wondered what it would be like to live on Mars. He imagined that he might see a note on the school bulletin board Monday that said, *Wanted: Boys to live on Mars for one month. Girls need not apply.* He would go. He would be first in line. He would come back to earth just as the horrible month of being slaves to the Malloys was up.

He tried to think of a costume to end all costumes. He remembered how the Hatfords and Bensons had once painted black stripes on their white T-shirts, chained themselves together, and walked in the parade as a chain gang. Another time they had all worn cardboard fronts and backs, painted black with white dots, and entered the contest as a set of dominoes. They had even been a fly swatter and bugs. Wally didn't see how the girls could ever come up with something better than that. They might, though. The only thing the boys could think of to do this Halloween was to go as "punkin' heads," with pumpkins cut out at the bottom so that Wally and his brothers could slip their heads up inside from underneath.

"What we need to do," he said, almost to himself, "is spy on the girls and see what they're going to be. Just in case."

"I was thinking the same thing," said Josh, busily making a sketch of Caroline in the poncho, almost being tossed into the river. Josh took a sketchpad wherever he went. "One of us has to be a mole."

"A mole?" asked Wally.

"A spy from the inside out," said Jake, and they all turned toward Peter.

"What's the matter?" Peter asked warily. "Why are you looking at *me*?"

"How would you like to be a mole?" said Jake.

"The most important job you've ever had," added Josh.

"And if you goof up, we're dead meat," said Wally. He heard Peter swallow.

•

At school the next day there was not a notice on the bulletin board requesting boys to go to Mars. There was a sign-up sheet outside the principal's office for entering the Halloween contest. Some students wanted to be in the parade just for the fun of dressing up, but others wanted to be judged on their costumes. If you wanted to be judged, you were supposed to put your name on the sign-up sheet and say whether you were coming as a group or as an individual.

Jake saw the sign-up sheet first, and right there at the top, under group entry, he wrote: *The Hatfords: Jake, Josh, Wally, and Peter.*

By lunchtime there was another entry on the sheet under "group": *The Malloys—Eddie, Beth, and Caroline.*

It was official. This time *Wally* swallowed.

"Think!" said Jake when the boys got home. "What excuse can we think of to send Peter over there to look around?"

"Maybe he could ask Caroline about your homework assignment, Wally," said Josh.

"Are you nuts?" said Wally. "She's the last person I'd ask, and she knows it."

"Peter could ask to borrow a cup of sugar," said Jake.

Josh wrinkled his nose. "That's about the phoniest excuse there is."

Everybody looked at Wally.

"He could return Caroline's sock," Wally said.

"Bingo!" said Jake and Josh together.

They sat Peter on the kitchen table, gave him half a Hershey bar that Jake had been carrying around in his pocket, and went over his instructions.

"Here's what you do," said Jake. "You go up to

the Malloys' front door and ask for Caroline. When she comes to the door, give her the sock and tell her you were worried about whether she got home okay."

"I was?" asked Peter.

"Well . . . sure. I mean, we were all wondering . . . uh . . . sort of . . . whether the girls got home all right in the rain," said Jake. "We didn't want them to get wet, did we?"

"You were ready to throw her in the *river*!" Peter said.

"Oh, not really. Just trying to scare her a little," Josh told him.

"She'll probably make some nasty remark, but just ignore her. Keep saying you were worried, and here's her sock, and then ask if they could give you any ideas of what you could be in the Halloween parade," Jake told him.

"No, I've got it!" said Josh. "Tell them we won't let you be in the parade with us, and you want to be in the parade with them. They probably won't let you, but if you pay attention, they'll probably give some clue about what their costume is going to be."

Peter's face clouded up and Wally began to feel very uncomfortable.

"But I *can* be in the parade with you, can't I?"

"Sure, but you're just saying that so—"

"Then it's a lie," Peter said flatly.

"No, it's not, Peter, because right now I'm telling you that you can't be in the parade with us, but after you come back from the Malloys, I'll tell you that you can."

"But—"

"Just *do* it, Peter! Just take Caroline's sock and see what you can find out."

"I always have to do everything!" Peter grumbled, yanking the sock out of Jake's hand, sliding off the table, and banging out the door.

Jake and Josh and Wally looked at each other.

"What do you bet he doesn't do it?" said Jake.

"He'll probably just drop the sock in the river and say he couldn't find out anything," said Josh.

"I'm going to follow along behind him just in case," Wally said, moving over to the window. He waited until Peter had got as far as the swinging bridge, then slipped out the door himself.

Since the Malloys had come to Buckman, nothing was the same, Wally thought, hands in his jacket pockets. He and his brothers couldn't even enjoy Halloween without worrying what the girls would wear in the parade. Just when he thought maybe they could forget the girls for a change, he had to worry what it would be like to lose the contest to Eddie, Beth, and Caroline and have them boss him around for a whole month. That was about the stupidest bargain Jake had ever made. It was dumber than dumb.

Up ahead, Peter was in no particular hurry to get to the Malloys'. He was placing the heel of one foot against the toe of the other, and he must have been counting with every step, because every so often he slapped the sock against the cable handrail and said, "Ten!" More steps. "Twenty! . . ."

Wally waited until his younger brother was across the bridge and had disappeared behind the trees on the other side before he went across himself. He quickened his steps as he reached the end because he wanted to make sure he was there in the bushes when Peter knocked on the door.

When Wally stepped off the end of the bridge, however, he paused, with one foot in the air, because Peter was not five yards away from him, stooping to fill Caroline's sock with stones.

Wally let out his breath. At this rate Peter would reach the Malloy house about midnight! He started to say something, then realized Peter probably wouldn't go up to the house at all if he knew Wally was watching, so he stood motionless, waiting, until Peter stood up and trudged on again, holding the bulging sock in one hand and whirling it around and around above his head.

When he came to the picket fence next to the Malloys', Peter dragged the sock along it . . .

whumpity, whumpity, whump . . . and began singing at the same time: "This old man, he played one, *he* played *knick*knack *on* my *thumb* . . ." And when he reached the end of the Malloys' driveway, Peter stopped and sang the next verse of the song holding his nose: "This old man, he played two, he played knickknack on my shoe . . ." When that was done, he pulled his bottom lip out away from his teeth and sang the third verse like that.

Wally didn't think he could stand it. He wondered if he should go grab the sock and try to find out something from Caroline himself, but he knew it would never work. Caroline would never, ever give him even the slightest clue about what the girls were going to be on Halloween. There was nothing to be done but wait it out.

At long last Peter sighed, straightened, dumped the stones out of the sock, and finally went up the driveway to the Malloys' front porch.

Wally crept along in the bushes by the side of the driveway, and finally made it up to the garage. He peeked around the corner.

Knock, knock, knock.

At first it didn't seem as though anyone was home. No one came to the door, and Peter even went over to a window and peeped in. He turned and started back down the steps. Wally wanted to yell, *Not yet! Try again!* when the door behind Peter opened.

"What do *you* want?"

Crazy Caroline herself!

"Uh . . . I—I . . ." Peter stammered.

"Well?"

Peter held out the sock. "I was worried about you," he said.

Good job! Wally thought. *Nice going, Peter!*

The irritation on Caroline's face gave way to surprise. "Why?"

"If you got home okay."

"Why were you worried about me when you were trying to throw me in the river? You weren't very worried then."

"I wasn't trying to throw you in the river. I was asleep in the tent," Peter told her.

Caroline's face softened immediately, and Wally wondered whether girls always felt motherly toward smaller children. Sisterly, anyway.

"Well, maybe you *were* in the tent. I couldn't see."

"All that was left of you was this sock," Peter went on in a small voice. Wally decided that if their family ever became poor, they could send Peter out to beg on street corners, because he obviously could wring your heart.

"Who is it, Caroline?" came a voice from inside.

"Peter Hatford. He found my sock."

"What?" Eddie stuck her head out the door, then came out on the porch, followed by Beth.

"He says he was worried about me. He was in the tent when his goon brothers tried to throw me in the river."

"They weren't really," Peter said. "They were only fooling."

"Now you tell me," said Caroline.

"But I was worried you might not find your way home in the rain," Peter plowed on.

Eddie studied him quizzically. "My, aren't we concerned all of a sudden," she said.

"I'm sure Josh and Jake and Wally were awake all night worrying about us," said Beth. "Nobody came over and offered to let us share your tent, though. If you ask me, Peter, I think you've got three baboons for brothers."

Wally strained to hear what they were saying next, but from where he stood behind the garage, he didn't think they were saying anything at all. Looking around the corner, it seemed to Wally as though the girls were whispering among themselves.

And suddenly he heard Eddie saying, "It was really nice of you to bring back Caroline's sock,

Peter. You want to come in for some peanut butter cookies?"

No, Peter, no! Wally thought desperately. *It's a trap! Don't do it! Don't go!*

But even as he thought it, he saw Peter's head bob up and down, and a moment later Peter disappeared into the Malloys' house, followed by Eddie, Beth, and Caroline, all three of them grinning.

Five

A Little Chat with Peter

It was the chance of a lifetime, and Caroline and her sisters knew it. Mother was at the dentist's, and they had Peter all to themselves. He was as gullible as a dry sponge; he'd soak up whatever they told him, but one squeeze, and he'd probably leak out all the Hatfords' secrets.

Beth and Eddie were thinking the same thing, because Peter had scarcely sat down at the kitchen table before there was an orange soda and a plate of cookies in front of him, with a little package of M&M's on the side.

"Tell me, Peter," said Eddie, "do your brothers *always* act like goons, or is it just around us?"

"Well, sometimes . . . I mean . . ." Peter seemed to be thinking it over, his mouth full of cookies. "Well, most of the time they're . . . Well, you know what? They won't even let me be in the Halloween parade with them, and I wanted to know if I could be in it with you."

Caroline knew a trap when she heard it. She could see it, smell it, and so could Beth and Eddie. The three girls exchanged looks. Actually, they had just that morning discussed the matter of a group costume, and decided to go as a centipede—three legs and three arms sticking out one side, three legs and three arms sticking out the other. Four arms and four legs would be even better, but how did they know Peter was telling the truth?

"Well, I don't know," said Beth. "We were planning to go as gypsies. Isn't that right, Eddie? I'm not sure you'd make such a good gypsy, Peter."

"Oh, yeah. Gypsies. Right!" said Caroline. "Sure you want to dress up in bracelets and stuff, Peter?"

"Huh-uh," said Peter, and took a long drink of orange soda.

Caroline sat down on one side of him. "Why won't your brothers let you be in the parade with them?"

"I don't know," Peter told her, and opened the package of M&M's.

Beth sat down on the other side. "I would think that *four* boys would have a better chance of winning the prize than three."

No answer.

Eddie tried next. "It's easy to think up a costume if you're a boy. All boys have to do is put on old clothes and be bums or something. They hardly have to do any work."

"Uh-*uh*!" said Peter. "We've got to cut holes in the bottoms of pumpkins for our heads to go through and—" He stopped, looking suddenly confused. Caroline and Eddie exchanged triumphant glances.

"Oh, I forgot!" cried Peter. "That was last year! Yeah, that's what we were *last* year. Punkin' heads. *This* year we're going as pirates. Yeah, *pirates*! I *forgot*!"

"Sure, Peter. Right. Pirates are a swell costume. I'll bet that'll win first prize," smiled Beth.

Looking much relieved, Peter grinned back and took another long drink of soda.

He was so cute that Caroline almost wished he were *her* little brother. At the same time it seemed foolish not to get all the information out of him that they could.

"Peter," she said, trying to sound as motherly as possible—if she were to become an actress, she would undoubtedly be asked, at some time in her life, to play the part of a mother—"tell me something; why do your brothers hate us?"

"They don't *hate* you," said Peter uncertainly. "They just don't like you very much."

"Oh, that makes me feel so much better!" said Beth.

"I mean, well, they *like* you, sort of, but . . . you're not boys!"

"How stupid of us!" said Eddie. "We're so sorry."

Peter plowed on. "It's just that we liked the Bensons better."

"Can *we* help it if the Bensons moved away?" Caroline asked. "Why take it out on us?"

Peter thought that one over too. "Well . . . see . . . if *you* go back to Ohio, and the Bensons can't find anybody to rent their house to, then maybe they'll come back."

"I get it," said Caroline. "Your baboon brothers think that if they make us miserable enough, we'll leave."

Peter nodded. "But *I* don't want you to be miserable."

"Of course not," said Eddie.

"You just want us to leave too," said Beth.

Peter reached for another cookie. "Well, not *exactly*, because . . . Wally doesn't want you to leave either."

Caroline was genuinely surprised. "He *doesn't*?"

"No. I mean, not yet. He said he wants you to stay in Buckman until we've done all the things we wanted to do to you and then . . . I mean . . . well . . ."

"Oh, we understand perfectly," said Beth.

Caroline sighed dramatically. "I guess we just can't win. No matter what we do, the boys will always get the best of us."

"Right," said Beth. "Pirates will always win a costume contest before gypsies. But I can't think of anything else to be, can you, Caroline?"

As Beth put the cookies back in the pantry, however, Caroline followed her in.

"Listen, Beth, are you *sure* we shouldn't try to get Peter to be in our costume with us? *Four* arms and legs would make an even better centipede, and he could be the tail."

"No. He'll give it away. Somehow he'd leak it to the others."

"Yes, but think how great it would be if we win first place and Peter was on our side! Like we'd recruited him right out from under their noses."

"Better to keep him as spy and not even let on that he is. No telling when we'll need him again," said Beth.

They went back in the kitchen where Peter was finishing his drink, and when he put his glass down he had a wide orange mustache above his upper lip.

"Thanks for bringing back my sock, Peter. Come over anytime," Caroline told him.

"Okay," Peter said, and after he went outside, he shuffled down the driveway, stopping to pick up an acorn, then another and another, filling his pockets with them, and skipping on.

"Too bad he's a Hatford," said Beth, watching.

But Eddie disagreed. "It's *great* he's a Hatford. Don't you realize what a coup this is! A spy in their own camp! I'm *sure* those guys are going as punkin' heads. They sent Peter over here to make us believe they were going as pirates, and he let the cat out of the bag. This is more fun than I thought."

"You know what's going to happen, though, don't you? They'll win!" said Beth. "Four guys with pumpkins on their heads will win over a centipede any day."

A glum silence settled down over the room.

"Then there's only one thing to do," said Eddie. "We've got to go over there before the parade and smash those pumpkins to bits."

"Eddie!"

Both Caroline and Beth looked shocked.

"That's playing dirty," said Beth.

"And they weren't? Sending Peter over here to try and find out what we were going to be on Halloween? And Peter's story about their being pirates? That was the lowest thing they could do."

"Still . . ."

"Still nothing! I'll smash their pumpkins myself."

"What if they keep the pumpkins in their house?"

"I doubt it. Once you carve a pumpkin it starts to stink if you keep it inside."

"We'd better make that centipede costume extra good just in case," said Caroline.

In a way, Caroline wished that they were going as something other than a bug. A centipede was okay, but she wished it could be something a bit more dramatic. An aspiring actress, she knew, was constantly on the lookout for life experiences that enabled her to practice a role, and she did not know of any plays or movies that would require her to play the part of a centipede. Still, if she were the *head* of the centipede instead of the tail . . .

"Could I be the head?" she asked her sisters. "I mean, maybe we could tell a little story. Maybe the head of the centipede always wants to go one way but the tail wants to go another. Or maybe the head of the centipede could be crying, and—"

Eddie sighed. "Caroline, for gosh sake, do you have to turn everything into a catastrophe? Can't you just be a *bug* for once and—"

"Well, maybe she has a point," said Beth. "It's got to be a pretty unusual centipede to win first prize."

Back in Ohio their school did not have contests. There was a Halloween party every year, but no parade around the business district, and no prizes for best costume. Caroline had dreaded moving to West Virginia because she thought it would be all mountains and cabins and coal mines, and here was a town with a college and a river and a swinging bridge and, best of all, an elementary school with an auditorium and stage.

An auditorium with a stage and a thick velvet curtain—gold on one side, maroon on the other. Caroline knew, she was utterly convinced, that someday she would perform on that stage, and it wouldn't be as a centipede either.

The door opened and Mother came in. She looked the same, but sounded different. And when she poured a glass of water and tried to drink, water trickled out one side of her mouth.

"Novocaine," she said, with a laugh. "I can't feel a thing." She looked around the kitchen at the empty glass and the cookie crumbs on a plate. "Looks like you've had a party."

"A little welcoming party," said Beth dryly.

"For whom?"

"Peter Hatford was by to pay us a visit," said Caroline.

"One of the Hatford boys? How nice! You know, I think our two families got off on the wrong foot somehow," Mother told them. "One of these days I'm going to bake them a pie to thank those boys for washing our windows. I think that would be a friendly gesture, don't you?"

Caroline, Beth, and Eddie exchanged looks.

"Maybe," said Caroline. "Maybe not."

Six

Birds of Prey

Peter had just stepped off the end of the bridge when three sets of hands grabbed him and he let out a squeal.

"What happened?" asked Wally. "What happened after you got inside?"

Peter licked at the rim of orange soda around his mouth. "We had a party," he said grandly, and kept walking.

Jake and Josh moaned.

"What *happened*?" Wally asked again.

"Well," said Peter, crossing the road, the boys keeping step beside him, "first we sat down in the kitchen, and Eddie poured me some orange soda, and then Beth got out the cookies, and—"

"Never mind the *food*, Peter, what *happened*?" Wally was beside himself.

"Let me *tell* it, Wally! And then Caroline gave me some M&M's and—"

"Those were bribes, Peter. Couldn't you tell?"

"They were *good*!" Peter went up on the porch. "And then Caroline asked why we hated them."

"She did? Caroline thinks we *hate* them?"

"And I said we didn't hate them, we just wanted them to stay long enough for us to do all the stuff we wanted to do to them and—"

Jake sank down on the steps. "We're dead," he said.

"We should never have let Peter go by himself," agreed Josh.

"Peter," said Wally, trying his best to be patient, "tell me the truth. Did you tell them we were going to be punkin' heads in the parade?"

"No! I told them that's what we were *last* year."

Jake and Josh groaned again.

"I told them that *this* year we were going to be pirates."

"But did you find out what *they* are going to be?" Wally asked.

This time Peter actually beamed. "I found out a secret!"

"What?" cried his three brothers at once.

"Well, *they* said they were going to be gypsies in the parade."

"Gypsies? They told you that?"

"That's what they said, but when Caroline and Beth went in the pantry, I heard them talking, and Caroline said they were going to be . . ." Peter's face blanched suddenly. "I—I forgot!"

This time Jake dramatically tumbled down the steps and lay stretched out on the sidewalk below. "I can't stand it."

Wally grabbed Peter by the shoulders. "Peter, a whole month depends on this—who's going to be boss, them or us."

"Um . . ." said Peter thoughtfully.

"What letter did it begin with? Can you even remember that?" pleaded Jake.

"S," said Peter.

"Scarecrows?" guessed Jake.

"No."

"A salad bowl—carrots and onions and stuff?" guessed Wally.

"Not something to eat." Peter frowned.

"Sheep?" asked Jake. "Sheep and shepherd?"

"No. Not an animal."

Wally was desperate. He would rather jump off the bridge than be the Malloys' slave for a month. He tried to think of everything he knew that began with an *s:* "Soap, sewing basket, spit, sandwich, shoes, stockings, snakes, soccer, slugs, slime . . ."

Peter's face lit up suddenly: "I know! It crawls!"

"Okay," Jake said excitedly. "We're getting close. It crawls, but it's not an animal."

"No. It's a—a bug. I think."

"Spider!" shouted Wally.

"No . . . it's got a lot of legs," Peter told them.

"A centipede?" Wally asked.

"Yes! That's it! A centipede!" Peter cried delightedly.

"That begins with a *c*, dope," said Jake.

"Never mind, we got it! A centipede, huh?" said Josh. "Oh, boy, how are we going to top that?"

"Think, Wally!" Jake said, as he always did when they needed an idea. "What could top a centipede? You know how the principal's always saying we should act the part—witches should act spooky and scarecrows should walk stiff-legged and soldiers should march and everything? What could mess up a centipede just by acting its part?"

Everyone looked at Wally.

"A giant boot," said Wally.

It was a good idea except that no one knew how four boys could be a giant boot, and even if they were, how could it come down on top of the girls, and even if it did, what was the good of that when they'd be expelled from the parade, not to mention school?

"Think some more," said Jake.

"A fly swatter," said Wally.

That had the same problems as a giant boot.

Wally tried to put his mind in the Destructo Mode. *Stamp, swat, squash, smash, swallow* . . .

Swallow!

"What eats insects?" he said aloud. "Birds. We could be birds."

"Birds?" asked Jake, not at all sure. "Who wants to be in a Halloween parade dressed as sparrows or something?"

"Not sparrows," said Wally, and suddenly he began to smile. "What about some big, horrible repulsive bird? What about vultures?"

"That's *it*!" cried Jake. "We're a flock of vultures! And right in the middle of the parade we'll descend on the centipede and tear its skin off."

Peter looked alarmed.

"Oh, we're not going to hurt anyone," said Jake. "All we'll do is play the part of a vulture and pull off the girls' costume. If anyone bawls us out, we'll say we were acting the part."

Peter's chin trembled a little. "They gave me cookies," he said.

Wally sat down beside him. "Listen, Peter, would you like it if every time you were on a swing at school, Caroline told you to get off so she could have it?"

"N-no."

"What if Eddie made you come over and clean her room? Or do their dishes? Don't you see what would happen if the girls win first prize and we have to be their slaves?"

"I guess."

"That's why we've got to be vultures," Jake told him. "Wally, find out everything you can about vultures."

•

The library was open on Monday nights, so after dinner Wally rode his bike over to the corner of East Main Street and Sedgwick. He looked up *vulture* in the encyclopedia. It didn't tell him much he didn't already know.

"Try our new *Birds of Prey* book," the librarian suggested, and pointed to a shelf under the window.

Wally found the book and sat down with his paper and pencil. He started reading and his eyes grew wide. He read some more and his mouth fell open. He could not believe what was there on the page.

A half hour later he was on his way home again, pedaling as fast as he could. Mom and Dad were out in the garden by the side of the house, picking the last of the tomatoes before they were killed by frost. Peter was on the living-room floor, building something with his Lego set, and Jake and Josh had their books spread out on the dining room table, doing their math assignment, when Wally burst through the front door.

"You are absolutely not going to *believe* this!" he told them. Peter got up and came over.

"Did you find out a lot of stuff we could do in the parade? Vulture stuff?" asked Jake.

"Hoo boy!" said Wally. He unfolded the piece of paper he had scribbled on at the library. "Number one," he read. "Vultures can soar as high as 26,000 feet."

"I'll do that one," Jake joked.

"They have a six-foot wingspan."

"Get real," said Josh.

"They eat road kill," Wally went on.

"That's you, Josh," said Jake.

"But their favorite food is rotting fish guts."

"That's you, Jake," said Josh.

"When they're scared, they throw up."

"That's you, Wally," laughed Jake and Josh together.

"And they cool themselves by peeing on their legs."

"That's Peter!" they all said at once.

"That's *not*! I won't do it! You always try to make me do everything!" Peter bellowed.

"But that's not the worst," Wally told them. "When the vulture is *really* upset, it . . . well, doo-doos. *Vigorously.*"

"How are we supposed to do all that in the Halloween parade?" asked Jake.

"Well, I don't know, but here's what we'd look like," said Josh, turning his paper over. "Maybe if we made some beaks out of papier-mâché, and some feet with claws . . ."

He immediately set to work.

•

At school the next day Wally was very, very careful not to act as though he knew that the Malloy girls were going to be a centipede. He was very, very careful not to even say the word *centipede.* Even when Caroline Malloy, who sat behind him, got restless in geography as she usually did and began bumping the back of his chair with her knees, he didn't even turn around.

When school was out that afternoon, he sat on the steps in the crisp October sunshine, collar turned up around his neck, and waited for Jake and Josh to come out. He was watching one lone leaf as it dangled from a branch above, twisting this way and that in the wind, and Wally wondered what it was like to be a leaf. Did it stay on the tree until its stem was dry and withered, then drop, or did it just suddenly think to itself one day, *That's it; I'm tossing in the towel,* or did it—

Suddenly the door banged again and out came Josh, his head down, Jake close at his heels.

"Gosh *darn* it!" Josh yelped, throwing his jacket on the ground. Then he picked it up and threw it again.

"What's wrong?" asked Wally.

"We had to trade papers for math and grade each other's," Jake explained.

"So?"

"So Josh had to trade with Eddie."

"So?" Wally said again.

"Eddie found the picture of the vulture that Josh drew on the back of his math paper," Jake told him.

Seven

Change of Plans

"You won't *believe* this!"

Eddie was waiting when Caroline and Beth came out of the building at three o'clock. The Hatford boys were already far down the sidewalk, their shoulders hunched against the wind.

"What?" cried Caroline.

"You won't *believe* it!" Eddie said again. "If you ever thought the Hatford boys might really be nice underneath, or kind, or polite, think again."

"What did they *do*?" insisted Beth.

"It's not what they did, it's what they were planning to do."

"*What?*" Caroline shouted. "Tell us!"

"I can't. Some things just have to be shown."

When they walked in the house, they all said hi to Mother, who was making a corn husk wreath to go on the front door, and went straight up to Eddie's room, which looked like the locker room of the New York Mets, because there were baseball pictures everywhere.

"Look." Eddie threw her books on the bed and sat down. Then, reaching into her jacket pocket, she pulled out a folded piece of paper. "I was supposed to give this back to Josh after I graded it, but I didn't."

Caroline leaned over and stared at the paper. "It says, *Math, 4 wrong.*"

Eddie turned the paper over. Caroline looked again. In the center of the picture was a drawing of a small centipede. There were three legs and three arms sticking out one side of it, three legs and three arms sticking out the other. And hovering over the centipede were four large ferocious-looking vultures, who were holding it down with their claws.

"They know!" Beth gasped.

"More than that," said Eddie. "*They're* going as vultures! Or *were.* But read the fine print."

Caroline looked hard at the first vulture.

Jake, it said above the vulture's head, and then, printed along the side: *Eats rotten fish guts. Josh,* it said above the second vulture: *Throws up on the centipede.*

"Gross!" cried Beth.

"It gets worse," said Eddie.

"Wally," read Caroline aloud, pointing to the third vulture. She studied the dotted line from the vulture to the centipede, then turned the paper sideways to see what this vulture was doing. *"Pees* on the centipede!" She stared aghast, but Beth snatched the paper away.

"Peter," she read. "Peter . . . doo—" She gasped. "Peter does the doo-doo."

"They wouldn't!" cried Caroline.

"I don't know what they'd do, but I never met four more disgusting guys in my life," said Eddie.

They sat motionless on the bed, staring at each other.

"So much for the centipede," said Beth.

"I wouldn't be a centipede for anything in the world," said Caroline.

"Then *think*!" said Eddie. "What *are* we going to be in the parade? We've got to be a bunch of something."

"Bananas?" said Caroline.

"It's been done."

"M&M's?"

"Everybody does that. Last year there were two groups of M&M's at our school back home. It's not original enough."

"One of us could be the Energizer rabbit, and the other two could be batteries," said Caroline.

Eddie sighed in disgust.

"How about if I go as a tube of Cheez Whiz, and you two go as crackers?"

"Thanks a lot," said Beth.

"Two dogs and a fire hydrant?" suggested Caroline, amazed at her own creativity.

"Not bad," said Eddie.

"A parking meter and two coins?"

"Keep going."

They thought of a toothbrush and molars, or Oxy pads and zits, but when they thought about how to make the costumes it just got too complicated.

"The point is," said Eddie, "the principal will be the judge. What *we* might like, and what the principal might like, are two different things entirely. It should probably be something with a lesson to it."

"Ugh." Caroline clutched her throat.

"I know, I know, but we've *got* to win first prize, Caroline. Do you want to be the Hatfords' slaves? Think what will happen if we lose! Do we really want to wash their socks and clean their bathtub and take out their trash every week?"

It was a distressing thought.

"What does the principal like?" asked Caroline.

"Trees," said Beth. "He really likes trees.

Somebody told me that every spring, he plants a tree at the end of the school yard."

"And did you ever read the poem he has framed above his bookcase? 'I think that I shall never see, a poem lovely as a tree . . .' " said Caroline dramatically.

"Okay," said Eddie. "We'll go as a shrub, with sticks taped to our arms for branches. Each of us will be a limb—a large limb. We'll be bound together at the waist and knees, so our legs form a thick trunk, but we'll each sort of spread our arms and wave them slowly in the wind. The principal will love it."

•

When Caroline woke the next morning, she had no idea that this would be one of the most wonderful days of her life, and it had nothing to do with a shrub.

"And now, class," the teacher said after she took the roll, "for those of you who are new at Buckman this year, we have a tradition you may not know about. Every spring the sixth grade puts on a play for the rest of the school"—Carolyn's heart sank. Only the *sixth* grade?—"but every October the fourth grade puts on a Halloween play for the lower grades."

Joy in the morning!

"It's not a very long play, because small children can't sit still very long, so there won't be a lot to memorize, but I think you'll find it fun."

Carolyn felt as though she were floating above the desks.

"This year I have selected *The Goblin Queen* for our play. As I read each part, if you think you would be interested, please raise your hand. First, the queen herself—"

Caroline's hand was in the air before the words had even left the teacher's mouth.

"Caroline?" said the teacher. "Is that all?"

Two more hands went up.

"Caroline, Nancy, and Kim," the teacher said. "You'll try out at lunchtime, girls, and we'll see who reads it best."

Caroline *was* floating. *She* could read it best. She knew she could.

"Three witches . . ." the teacher went on.

More hands went up, and the teacher wrote more names on the board.

"A grandfatherly ghost . . . a black cat . . . two skeletons . . ." The list went on and on, and more names were added. Wally didn't volunteer for a thing, Caroline noticed, but she didn't care.

After lunch she sat in a little circle by the teacher's desk, and one by one she and Nancy and Kim read the lines that the Goblin Queen would say. Caroline wonderfully, gloriously, deliriously outdid the other girls. Even Nancy and Kim had to admit it. "Caroline did it best," they said.

"Well, you two girls will be her goblins-in-waiting, then," Miss Applebaum said, "and those are good parts too. You are all good readers."

"Will the play be in the auditorium?" Caroline asked breathlessly. "Up on stage . . . with the velvet curtain and everything?"

The teacher looked amused. "Yes, Caroline, at long last, it will be up on stage in the auditorium with the velvet curtain and everything. The seats won't be filled, of course, only the first few rows, but it will be an appreciative audience. Everyone looks forward to the Halloween play."

•

When Caroline walked out of school that day, she came down the steps slowly, her back straight, head high, as a queen would walk as she stepped off the throne to greet her subjects.

"What's the matter, Caroline, a crick in your neck?" asked Eddie.

"You," said Caroline, "are looking at the actress with the leading role in the fourth-grade play, *The Goblin Queen.*"

"Gobble the Queen?" teased Beth.

Caroline gave her a haughty glance.

"I was the very best one in tryouts, and I will perform onstage!" And then she couldn't contain herself. She grabbed her sisters by the arms and dissolved in happy giggles. "Oh, Eddie! Beth! I'm so excited. We really get to be onstage, with the curtain and everything!"

"Well, just don't let it go to your head, Caroline," Eddie told her. "We've still got our costume to be working on, because if we don't win that contest, *Wally's* going to be king and you're going to be his loyal subject. And if that's not enough to make you throw up, I don't know what is."

Caroline sighed. "Ugh. What should we be doing?"

"We should be finding sticks to tape to our arms. Not too heavy, though, or our arms will get tired."

When the girls got across the swinging bridge, they went down the bank on the other side, where there were low-hanging branches, and looked for sticks that had fallen on the ground.

"I've got two, with lots of twigs on them," said Caroline, holding them up in the air. "How do these look, Eddie?"

Beth held hers up, too, to see if they would be too heavy.

"Do we look like a tree?" she asked.

"A good-sized shrub, maybe," said Eddie. She

stood on tiptoe to break off a long branch that was already dangling and added it to the others. "I think this will do it," she said at last.

"What are we going to call our costume in the contest?" asked Caroline. "Just 'shrub'?"

"Something that will appeal to the principal," Eddie said. She thoughtfully chewed her lip. "*I've* got it. 'A natural habitat'! That's what we'll call ourselves."

By the time they had put the sticks in the garage, Mother was standing at the door waiting for them: "I've made a pie for the Hatfords, and I want you girls to take it over," she said. "Just give it to whoever answers the door. Tell them it's in appreciation for the boys washing our windows. I've put it in this old hatbox and stuck a note inside."

"You've got to be kidding," said Eddie.

"Why would I be kidding?" Mother looked at her curiously. "You know, there are times I think I haven't raised you girls right. Maybe people just aren't as neighborly in Ohio, but here in West Virginia you show people you're grateful when they do something for you. It's the least we can do."

"I'll bet they throw it in the river," murmured Caroline.

"Throw it in the river! Why in the world would they do that?"

Caroline didn't even get a chance to tell Mother she was to be Goblin Queen in the fourth-grade play, because moments later she was crossing the swinging bridge, her sisters beside her, carrying the old hatbox with Mother's pumpkin chiffon pie inside it.

Eight

Pumpkin Chiffon

"Look!" said Josh.

Wally looked where his brother was pointing. On the bank, across the river, Caroline and her sisters were down by the water gathering sticks.

The boys moved behind some wild rhododendron and watched.

"What do you suppose they're up to?" asked Jake.

Josh turned to Wally. "Your class isn't doing a project with sticks, is it?"

Wally shook his head.

"Maybe they're going to have a fire in their fireplace," suggested Peter.

"The Bensons left them stacks and stacks of wood," Jake told him. "This has got to be something else. What do you think, Wally?"

Wally watched the girls without answering. He

watched them holding the sticks up in the air, sort of like poles for a tepee.

"A tepee," he said.

"That's *it*!" cried Jake. "Wally, you're a genius! They're going to come to the Halloween parade as a tepee and Indians! Eddie will probably be the tepee and Beth and Caroline will be the chief and squaw."

"Wow!" said Peter admiringly.

Wally felt sick. The Malloys would win for sure. *No*body had ever entered the parade before as a tepee and Indians. How could they ever top that?

"How can we top that?" asked Josh.

"We don't *have* to top it!" Jake answered. "All we have to do is stop it. All we have to do is dress up like something that would naturally knock down a tepee. *Think*, everybody!"

"A train?" said Peter.

"Not a train, dum-dum."

"A car?"

"Peter, we're talking Old West here, way back before there *were* any cars. C'mon, Wally. What could it be?"

Wally tried to remember pictures he'd seen in his history book, in the chapter called "Westward, Ho!"

"Buffalo," he said.

"That's it!" cried Jake. "We're buffalo. We don't have to be vultures after all. Josh, you've got to design some new costumes."

The boys went on home and made milk shakes in the kitchen to celebrate.

"I didn't *think* they'd be a centipede," Josh said. "I'll bet they whispered that just loud enough for Peter to hear so it would throw us off. They probably knew already they were going to be a tepee and Indians."

"All this time they've probably been working on their costumes—the chief's headdress and everything—while we were trying to find something that looked like vultures' claws," said Josh.

Ding dong.

Jake had just turned off the blender and was pouring the thick shake into glasses when the doorbell rang.

"Don't anybody take a drink of mine," Wally warned as he went to the door and opened it.

There stood Caroline and her sisters holding a hatbox.

"Mom sent this over," Caroline said, holding out the box. "It's a pumpkin pie."

Wally could not believe this was happening. The girls didn't look as though they liked this any more than he did, but Wally couldn't be sure.

"Who is it, Wally?" called Jake.

"A pie," said Wally.

"Who?"

Peter came running to the doorway and stared down through the cellophane top of the hatbox. "It's a pumpkin pie!" he said.

"Enjoy," said Eddie, and the girls turned and walked away.

"Don't forget to return the plate," Beth called over her shoulder.

All four boys were standing at the door now.

"I don't think their mom baked this at all," said Josh. "I'll bet there's a trick to it."

"That's what they thought when they threw our cake in the river," Wally reminded him.

"Just the same, I'll bet it's made of dog doo or something. I'll bet the girls are ticked off because of what I drew on the back of my math paper." Josh stared hard at the pie.

Wally opened the lid and took a cautious sniff. "Sure doesn't smell like dog doo."

"I still think there's something gross in it. Like centipedes. Bugs of some kind."

They took the pie to the kitchen and Wally lifted it out of the box. He accidentally let go of one side too soon, and it fell to the table with a plop. A large crack appeared on the top of the pie.

"Hoo boy!" said Wally.

"It's okay. That will give us a chance to see if

there's anything in the middle of it," said Jake. He got out Mother's magnifying glass and held it over the crack in the pie.

"See anything?" asked Wally.

"Not yet. Give me a butter knife."

Wally handed him a knife, and Jake probed gently down into the crack, then pulled the knife out and looked at the pumpkin coating it. "Looks okay, but I wouldn't be too sure."

"They probably wouldn't have stuck anything right in the middle of it," Josh said. "If I were going to put something gross in a pie, I'd stick it along the edge of the crust where you wouldn't think to look."

Jake took the knife and probed every few inches near the edge of the pie. With a spoon he lifted out a little bit of pumpkin chiffon here and a little there, examining it closely. It appeared to be only pumpkin.

"We still ought to taste it," he said. "It still could be made with pee. Who wants the first taste?"

"Not me!" said Wally.

"Don't look at me," said Josh.

Everyone turned to Peter.

"You always make me do everything!" Peter wailed.

"Oh, I'll take the first bite," said Jake. He lifted

the spoon to his lips and touched it first with his tongue. Then he actually put some in his mouth and rolled it around a moment, swallowing. "I'll be darned," he said. "It's good."

"Let me see," said Josh. Another bite. "You're right. It's great!"

"Give me some," said Peter, jabbing a spoon down right in the middle and lifting out a large bite.

And then Wally saw the note stuck to the bottom of the box. "Oh, no!" he said.

Dear Ellen—

Just wanted you to know how much we appreciated your boys washing our windows. There is such a wonderful sense of community here. Thank you so much for helping us to feel at home. Hope you enjoy my pumpkin chiffon pie—it's my great-aunt's recipe, and sort of a tradition at our house in October.

Cordially,

Jean Malloy

"Oh, brother!" said Josh.

"We," added Jake, "are in big trouble."

They stared down at the pie, which looked as though squirrels had been walking through it in golf shoes. Bites had been taken out of it here and there.

"Mom will *kill* us if she sees this!" said Wally. Mother always said that a gift of food should be enjoyed three ways: first with the eyes, then with the nose, and finally, with the mouth. If someone went to all the work to bake something for you, you should admire it first as an artistic creation, and not just gobble it down.

"What are we going to tell her?" Josh murmured.

"That we were digging for dog doo?" said Peter.

"There's only one thing to do," Jake decided. "Eat the pie. Then we've got to go to Ethel's Bakery and buy another. We'll put it in the box with the note and leave it on the table, and Mom won't know the difference. We'll take the plate back to Mrs. Malloy and tell her that Mom said thanks."

The boys ate the pie, more out of duty than pleasure—not because it wasn't good, but because they didn't seem so hungry anymore.

Afterward, Wally went upstairs to shake money out of his bank and wondered how life could get so complicated. Unfortunately, all the money he had was in a clay piggy bank that Aunt Ida had given him last Christmas, and the only way anyone could get money out was to shake it upside down and hope that something would fall out of the slot, though it hardly ever did.

He sat on his bed and shook and shook. How could it be that with so many dimes and nickels and pennies in it, hardly any ever hit the slot in exactly the right way to fall out? If one coin fell out every ten minutes, and there were a hundred and seventy-nine coins, then how long would it take before . . . ?

"*Hurry,* Wally! We have to be home in a half hour. We need to buy that pie before Mom gets here, and we've only got five dollars between us. We'll need more than that."

Wally took a hammer, smashed his clay piggy bank to smithereens, scooped up the money, and gave it to Jake.

•

The boys were all in the other room quietly watching TV when their mother walked in the back door and clunked her purse and keys on the kitchen counter.

"What's this?" Wally heard her say.

There was a silence—a long, long silence. The sound of a box being opened. The squeak of the kitchen floor. Then a long, slow "I de-clare!"

Wally held his breath.

"I de-clare!" Mother said again.

Wally couldn't stand it. Neither could Jake or Josh or Peter. They all went to the door of the kitchen.

"Well, now I've seen everything!" Mother said, staring down into the box and holding Mrs. Malloy's note in her hand.

"I don't see anything," said Wally.

"Did this just come this afternoon?" Mother asked, pointing to the box.

Wally nodded. "Caroline and her sisters brought it over."

Mother stood shaking her head. "Jean Malloy says in her note that she baked this pumpkin chiffon pie herself from her great-aunt's recipe, and this pie came from Ethel's Bakery, or I'll eat the box."

Wally almost choked.

"H-how do you know?" asked Jake.

"Because Ethel's the only one who sprinkles caramel and pecans around the rim of her pumpkin pies. And what's more, she always leaves a little swirl of filling right in the middle, sort of a trademark, you might say. I saw these pies in her window just this morning, and Jean Malloy's got the nerve to tell me she made it herself."

Hoo boy! Wally thought, and his legs felt like rubber. Maybe they should tell her. Maybe they should just come right out and tell her that when she sent that chocolate cake over to Mrs. Malloy in August, Caroline thought it was a trick and threw it in the river, so the boys thought maybe this was a trick, and they were just trying to dig around and see if there was any dog doo in it. . . . But then he thought of how awful Mom would feel if she knew her beautiful cake had gone in the river. She'd want to know *why* Caroline would suspect such a thing, and then he'd have to tell her all the ways the Hatford boys and the Malloy girls had been tormenting each other since the Malloys arrived. No, he had better keep quiet.

"If the woman doesn't bake, it's not a sin," Mother went on. "Why couldn't she just have said she'd picked up a pie for our dinner and hoped we'd enjoy it? Why did she have to say she baked it herself? And then, to call it pumpkin chiffon, when pumpkin chiffon pie is at least two inches high. If this is the way they do things in Ohio, I'm glad I don't live in Ohio. Boys, wash up. We're having dinner soon."

Nine

Thank-you Note

It was when Caroline was brushing her teeth the next morning that Wally returned the plate. She had been standing in front of the mirror practicing her lines for the play—"Wait, little elf. Maybe your idea is a good one! Maybe it *would* be more fun to do *good* tricks this Halloween and surprise the village people!"—when she heard the doorbell.

"Why, good morning, Wally!" came her father's voice. "Or is it Jake or Josh or Peter? I'm never sure."

"I'm Wally," came a second voice. "I just wanted to return Mrs. Malloy's pie plate and tell her thank you very much. The pumpkin chiffon pie was delicious!"

"I'll be sure to tell her," Father said. "Jean makes it every year. I like a big piece after a football game. Provided we win, of course."

Caroline came down after she heard the door close.

"Well, *now* maybe we're all friends again," Mother said to her. "One of the Hatford boys returned my pie plate and said the pie was delicious, so I guess they really enjoyed it. Let's try and keep things this way, huh? Stay friends?"

"Why not?" said Caroline. At the moment Wally and his brothers were the last thing on her mind. It was the play that was important. Never mind that the fifth and sixth grades wouldn't see it. The others would, along with all their teachers, and people would remember her, so that when they were looking for someone to play a starring role in fifth or sixth—

"Good grief! Have some bread with your peanut butter!" Mother said, watching Caroline make her lunch. "You have enough peanut butter on that bread for three sandwiches, Caroline. Pay attention."

"Dost thou talk to thy queen in such a manner?" Caroline asked, raising one eyebrow.

"I dost," said Mother. "And don't forget to pack some carrots and celery, m'lady."

•

"Well, class, we've got one week to the Halloween play," Miss Applebaum said, facing the fourth graders in her apple-red dress. "I still need three more boys, however, and if I don't get any volunteers, I'm going to have to volunteer for you. Come on, now. It'll be fun. Your audience is only little kids, after all. Don't let it scare you. If you forget a line, so what? It's not the end of the world."

Finally one hand went up, then another.

"Okay, I've got everyone we need except a footman, and we need somebody strong. Wally Hatford, I choose you. Lunch-hour rehearsal. Don't forget."

Wally Hatford! A footman! Right! thought Caroline.

When she stood on the stage at lunchtime, Caroline remembered that the last time she was here, having sneaked in after lunch, Wally and some of the other fourth-grade boys had sneaked in, too, unknown to her, and were sitting in the dark in the back row, listening to her read a beautiful passage from *The Wind in the Willows*. But now she was supposed to be here, with the lights shining down on her, and Miss Applebaum smiling in the second row, and sometimes, when Miss Applebaum was showing someone else where to stand, or how to gesture when he talked, Caroline tipped back her head and studied all the ropes and pulleys and lights and switches and knew that this was where she belonged, that she was doing what she was born to do.

There was only one line, at the very end of the play, where someone had a better part than Caroline. That was when the Fairy Godmother of All the Woods and Glades came to the Goblin Queen and said, "Isabelle, all these years your hair has been matted and your skin has been wrinkled and rough, and your toes and fingers crooked, because you have looked the way you have lived. But because of these fine deeds you have performed this Halloween, you have shown the village people that beneath your dirty hair and crooked smile, there is indeed a heart of gold." Whereupon she touched the Goblin Queen with her magic wand, and flung off the ugly mask that Caroline would have been wearing, to reveal the true beauty beneath.

For just that one moment Caroline would have liked to be the Fairy Godmother of All the Woods and Glades, but she couldn't be both. And besides, right after that, her two footmen were supposed to help her sit down, and say, "Your throne, m'lady." And when she said, "Call the other goblins, that we may celebrate a Halloween of Good Deeds," Wally would say, "I hear, my Queen, and obey."

When Wally came to those lines, however, his face turned red and he looked as though he had a mouth full of rocks. He looked as though he would rather choke than say them.

"Who are you talking to, Wally, the floor?" Miss Applebaum called from her seat in the second row. "Speak up—look at Caroline when you talk. Don't mumble."

"I can't remember the lines, I'm not any good at this," Wally told her.

"Pish-posh!" said their teacher. "You only have two lines to say in the whole play, Wally. Come on, now. I know you can do it. Besides, if you forget a line, just make one up. Actors and actresses have to do that all the time."

"I hear, my Queen, and obey," Wally said finally, and started off the stage to call the other goblins.

Does life ever get better than this? Caroline wondered happily.

•

Fall was perhaps the favorite season in the Malloy family. Father was happiest when football had really begun; Mother liked it when the long, hot days of summer were over at last; Eddie liked any season that was warm enough for her to stand outside and bounce a ball off the side of the garage; and Beth liked autumn especially because all the books that had been taken from the library for summer reading had been returned, and she had a much better selection to choose from, especially her favorite books, such as *The Spider's Sting, Mark of the Mummy,* and *Scorpion People.* But the seasons of the year meant absolutely nothing to Caroline as long as she was onstage.

She and Beth and Eddie had just come back from the homecoming parade on Saturday and were raking leaves when Mr. Hatford came up the sidewalk with their mail.

"Hello, girls," he said. "Your dad must have been mighty pleased the way his team beat Wheeling last night. Nice to have a winning team for a change." He grinned as he walked up the steps. "So how are you all doing?"

"Fine," they answered together.

Caroline took a chance: "How are the guys coming with their Halloween costumes?"

Mr. Hatford scratched his head. "Come to think of it, I haven't heard a word out of them the past few days. All I get from Wally is griping about some danged play."

Caroline grinned, but Eddie put down her rake: "Aren't they even going to *be* in the parade?"

"I imagine so. Just don't hear them talk much about it, that's all."

Not much help from him, Caroline thought after he had gone. Was it possible the boys had just given up?

Leaves fell down around them, and Caroline stretched her arms toward the sky and said, "Life's wonderful! The Goblin Queen is in her glory! I never want to go back to Ohio again. I want to stay right here and become known in Buckman, and someday, in the concrete outside the school, they will put a marker for me with my name on it, saying, CAROLINE LENORE MALLOY FIRST APPEARED ONSTAGE IN THIS SCHOOL." Her sisters groaned.

The screen door slammed and Mother came down the steps: "Girls, look at this and tell me what you think. I just got a note from Mrs. Hatford, and this is what she said:

'Dear Mrs. Malloy:

If you hadn't said you made that pie yourself, I would have sworn it came from Ethel's Bakery. Thank you so much. It was delicious.

Ellen Hatford'

Is that an insult or a compliment? I can't even tell."

"She thinks you bought the pie?" asked Eddie.

"It certainly sounds that way to me."

"So isn't that a compliment?" asked Caroline.

"Not to me it's not. Not when it was Great-

Aunt Minna's recipe. Maybe she's just trying to take me down a peg—my bragging on about that recipe as I did. Oh, dear heaven! People were so much easier to get along with back in Ohio!"

After Mother went back in the house, Beth whispered, "What do you think happened to the pie? You don't think they threw it in the river, do you?"

"Well, *something* happened to it, or they wouldn't have bought a store pie and tried to pass it off as homemade. I'm sure that's exactly what happened too," Eddie said.

"Maybe it was just so good that once they took a taste, they kept eating and couldn't stop," Caroline suggested.

"I doubt it," said Eddie.

•

At school on Monday, Caroline leaned forward and whispered, "Wal-ly. Mom wants her pie back."

Miss Applebaum was over in one corner helping a group with a geography assignment.

Wally turned around. "What?"

"She says that since you didn't give it to your mother, she wants it back."

Wally stared.

"Well?" said Caroline.

"Well, nothing! We ate it!"

"Your mother didn't."

"How do you know?"

"The Goblin Queen knows all."

"Drop dead," said Wally.

"If we win the costume contest, you'll have to say, 'I hear, my Queen, and obey,' for a whole month. Did you ever think of that?"

"And if *we* win . . . ?"

Miss Applebaum turned around. "I hear people talking. Is that you, Caroline? Caroline and Wally? Suppose you share it with the class."

"Just practicing our lines, Miss Applebaum," Caroline said sweetly.

Ten

The Grand Finale

The buffalo costumes were not working out. Even Josh, the artist in the family, could not make brown grocery sacks look like the shaggy heads of buffalo, no matter how much stuff he glued on them. Every time he changed them still again and showed them to Mother, she'd say, "Is that a goat? No, wait. I've got it—a sheepdog."

"Why don't we just forget the girls and do something we think will win?" said Wally.

But Jake had other ideas. "What we need is a costume the teachers will like and the principal will love, that can still destroy anything in its path. Then no matter *what* the Malloys come up with, we can devour it."

"*Think*, Wally!" said Josh. "Think of something that can sort of suck up everything in its path."

"A vacuum cleaner," said Wally.

"Naw. What else?"

"A tidal wave."

"Yeah, what else?"

"A tornado."

"Keep thinking."

"An amoeba," said Wally.

"C'mon, Wally, *think*!"

Wally closed his eyes tight and thought so hard, his eyebrows hurt. "An alien spaceship," he said at last.

"That's it!" cried Jake. "We'll be aliens!"

"They can do anything!" said Josh. "We could get one of those huge truck inner tubes, and all of us could stand inside the middle, holding it up around our waists, and we'd knock over everything we bumped into! I'll design our helmets. . . ." He reached for his sketch pad and began. All you had to do was give Josh an idea, and he was already drawing a picture of it in his head.

"Wow," said Peter softly, as he watched the alien spaceship appearing right at the end of Josh's pencil.

When they asked their dad if he could get a giant inner tube for them, Mr. Hatford answered, "Why, I think that could be arranged."

At last everything seemed to be working out. The Halloween parade was only four days off, but meanwhile Wally had another worry. The play. *The Goblin Queen.* Caroline Malloy, in particular.

The trouble with Caroline was that she never stopped being queen. If she was eating lunch, she set her empty milk carton on top of her head like a crown and kept it there. If she had to go to the blackboard to explain a problem, she always picked up Miss Applebaum's pointer and used it like a scepter, anointing a knight. And she would slowly, regally, make her way up and down staircases, back straight, head high, looking neither to the right nor left.

To Wally there was nothing worse than being in a play with Caroline Malloy. Never mind that he would be doing something special for the younger students. He did not *want* to make primary children happy. The primary children were happy enough as it was. Wally wanted his recesses back. He wanted his lunch hour back. He did not want to spend them standing around a drafty stage waiting for Caroline Malloy to decide that playing good tricks at Halloween was better than playing bad ones. Whoever wrote that play was an idiot. It took thirty minutes for the Goblin Queen to get the point and the Fairy Godmother to make her beautiful, just so Wally could say, "Your throne, m'lady," and then, "I hear, my Queen, and obey."

Each day of practice got longer and longer because Caroline kept ad-libbing her part. If her line was "What do you suppose, dear sisters, the villagers would do if we were to *wash* their windows for a change?" Caroline would say, "What do you suppose, my dear, dear goblin sisters, the villagers would do if, instead of causing them trouble and hardship, we did something kind instead, such as washing their windows?"

Wally would stand on one foot and then the other, and finally even Miss Applebaum grew tired: "Caroline, if we don't hurry this play along, our primary students will all be asleep before we're done."

And finally Caroline would say, "We must spread the word throughout the Goblin Kingdom, that there will be the kind of tricks on Halloween night that will make it a night to remember and fill all hearts with joy." Then and only then could Wally escort her to her chair and say, "Your throne, m'lady."

•

When Thursday came, Wally wasn't sure whether he wanted to get up or not. It was the day of the play, which was a good reason to stay in bed. On the other hand, once it was over, he'd never have to do that part again, which was the only reason he could think of to get up at all.

He turned over on his back and noticed a narrow shaft of sunlight coming through his window, illuminating the dust particles in the beam. It was as though the beam were full of dust and the rest of the room was clear. If air was always so dusty, he wondered, did you inhale a big wad of dust every time you breathed? Were your lungs like a dust mop? Was that why people sneezed, to shake out their lungs? Was that—?

"Wally, are you up?" Mother called from below. "If you want pancakes, you'd better come now."

Wally, the footman, got out of bed, pulled on his jeans and socks, and gave a big sigh.

At school the primary students filed into the auditorium about ten o'clock, and the students from Miss Applebaum's class who were in the play gathered behind the velvet curtain onstage.

"I can't believe this is really happening," Caroline said to Wally, both of them wearing their goblin cloaks and hoods. "I'm a real actress at last. Do you know where you'll see my name someday?"

"On a tombstone?" said Wally.

Caroline flashed him a disgusted look. "In lights! On Broadway! Someday you and your brothers will go to the movies and see me up there on the screen."

"If we see you on the screen, we'll ask for our money back," Wally told her.

Beyond the velvet curtain the audience had grown quiet, and Wally could hear Miss Applebaum telling them about the play. And then the music started, the lights went out, there was the sound of the curtain being pulled apart, and Caroline was walking onstage followed by five other goblins.

"Halloween again!" Caroline was saying. "I wish we could do something different this year, don't you? I'm getting tired of the same old thing." And the play began.

If it wasn't for Caroline, Wally might have enjoyed the play—a little bit, anyway. It was sort of fun peeping out from behind the curtain to see the younger children watching, Peter with his eyes wide and his mouth open. To hear them laugh at all the funny lines, and giggle when one of the witches tripped over her broomstick on purpose and went sprawling.

He and another boy had to pull the curtain between the first and second acts, too, and that was fun. It was also fun to watch the custodian sitting on a stool offstage, making the lights get brighter or more dim.

But Caroline, as usual, had to ruin it all. She added lines that weren't there. She added words to the lines that were. Even Miss Applebaum in the first row was trying to get Caroline's attention to hurry her along. Finally, when it came time for Wally to say his line, he felt he could not stand it any longer.

"Your throne, m'lady," he said, escorting her to the chair, and then, just as Caroline sat down, he pulled it backward and Caroline sat down on the floor with a plop.

The primary children shrieked with laughter, and even Miss Applebaum, who looked horrified at first, seemed to be trying very hard not to laugh.

Wally had thought that would be the end of it. He had thought that Caroline would be so embarrassed that she would want the play to be over quickly.

But Caroline was not hurrying her lines. She was not even getting up. The children stopped laughing. Miss Applebaum leaned forward, looking concerned.

And then, from the floor where she lay with her arms outstretched, Caroline said grandly, "Where are my good and faithful footmen? I am more exhausted than I knew. Please bear me thither, that I might lie among the flowers of the field, surrounded by my people." And she folded her arms across her chest.

Wally stared at Caroline and then at the other

footman. They looked at Miss Applebaum, who was nodding to them.

There was nothing else to be done. "I hear, my Queen, and obey," Wally said.

He picked Caroline up by the arms. The other footman picked her up by the feet. And as they carried her offstage, Caroline turned toward the audience and blew them a kiss. Everyone clapped. It made Wally sick to his stomach.

•

That evening the boys tried out their spaceship costume. Mr. Hatford had gone to a truck stop near Elkins and bought a bigger inner tube than the boys even knew existed. All four of them could easily fit in the center hole, one hand holding the inner tube up, the other carrying the space guns that Josh had designed out of aluminum foil. Each of them was facing a different direction, and with the strange helmets Josh had designed, also of foil, they looked like men from another planet. Josh had even made green paper ears that fit over their own.

"Well, if you don't win first prize, you should get a prize for originality," their father told them, as the boys practiced moving about the living room, two walking sideways, one walking backward, and Jake in front, leading the way. Naturally

Jake. It was Wally's idea, yet Jake was always the General.

When Mother came home from the hardware store at nine, the boys showed her their spaceship, and she said it was the best costume they'd ever made, absolutely.

As she hung up her coat, however, Wally heard her say to his father, "Tom, are the Malloys raising chickens?"

"Chickens? I'd think the coach would have enough to do without fooling with chickens. Why?"

"Because the Malloy girls were in the hardware store the other day buying chicken wire, and I just wondered."

"What?" yelled Wally, and slipped out from under the giant inner tube.

The other boys crawled out, too, and the inner tube landed with a loud *whap* on the floor.

Mrs. Hatford turned around. "Wally, don't yell. I simply asked if the Malloys were raising chickens."

Jake and Josh stared at her openmouthed.

"What did I *say*?" Mrs. Hatford looked around her. "It's not as though I announced the Second Coming! All I said was that the Malloy girls were in the store to—"

"How *much* wire?" asked Jake.

"Why, I don't know . . . quite a lot, as I remember, but it isn't our best grade at all. It was that bendable stuff that will sag if even a cat jumps on it."

"Their *costume*!" cried Wally.

"They aren't going to be a tepee at all, I'll bet!" said Josh. "Think, Mom! Did they buy anything else? *Say* anything? *Do* anything?"

"What's got into you boys? The youngest one stood there wrapping it around and around herself, while the older sisters were paying for it, but I figured she was just being a bit silly, and . . ."

The boys huddled around the kitchen table.

"What do you suppose it could be?" asked Josh.

"Something awesome, I'll bet," said Wally.

"There's only one thing to do," said Jake, when the others turned toward him. "Smash it."

Eleven

Izzie

The "natural habitat" had simply not worked. Murphy's Five and Dime didn't carry the little birds and things the girls had wanted to tie to the branches. And when Caroline, Beth, and Eddie were all bound together to make the trunk, it was hard to walk. They finally decided on a lizard made out of chicken wire.

"The principal has a terrarium in his office," Eddie remembered, "with a lizard and stuff. I even know the name of the lizard—Izzie, he calls it. Why don't we be a lizard and wear a collar that says IZZIE?"

So they bought some chicken wire at the hardware store, fashioned it into a huge lizard in three sections, one for each of them, then spent the evening before the parade tacking green cloth over it, using buttons for eyes, and printing IZZIE on a collar to go around its huge neck.

When Caroline awoke the next morning, she decided that life was more wonderful in Buckman than she had ever imagined. The day before, she had been a Goblin Queen, and today she was the hindquarters of a giant lizard. She made her parents laugh by waddling around in her part of the costume, sticking out one leg, then the other.

Coach Malloy carefully tied the lizard forms to the roof of his car and drove them to school. As the girls carried them in on their heads, they saw the Hatford boys stop in their tracks and stare.

"You guys still in the parade, or do you just want to give up now?" Eddie asked, as they arranged the sections in the proper order.

"Why don't you just promise to be our obedient slaves and get it over with?" said Beth.

"Whatever you've thought of, I'll bet it can't top this," said Caroline.

And she saw Peter look up at Wally. "We can't, can we?" he asked, and Caroline and her sisters smiled.

Why didn't the boys stop trying to drive them out of Buckman? Caroline wondered. That trick Wally had pulled on her during the play really backfired when he had to carry her out. *Everyone* had cheered for her. She was the Goblin Queen to end all Goblin Queens, and Wally had only created a scene that was even better.

"The contest isn't over yet," said Jake.

"It hasn't even started," Peter said.

"Don't count your chickens . . . uh, lizards . . . before they're hatched," said Wally.

•

It was hard to keep their minds on their studies that morning. Wally seemed nervous as a cat in a doghouse, Caroline thought, and it was strange to know that with a mother who worked in a hardware store, the Hatford boys couldn't have thought up something original themselves.

At noon the lunchroom was buzzing with chatter about the afternoon, and when the bell rang at one, all students who were going to enter the contest in groups were allowed to get ready.

Caroline went to the rest room, her last chance before she became a lizard, then hurried out into the hallway. She stopped, for there, disappearing around a corner, was a huge giant inner tube, propelled by the Hatford brothers, all wearing strange alien helmets and carrying space guns. The boys even had green paper ears. It was a *wonderful* costume! They'd win for sure.

No sooner had the aliens disappeared, however, than Eddie came racing down the hall, fire in her eyes.

"Where are they?" Eddie was saying, Beth at her heels. "Where are they?"

"Who?"

"The Hatford goons, that's who," said Eddie. "Did you see what they did to Izzie?"

Caroline ran down the hall and looked. Izzie the Lizard was flat as a slice of cheese.

"Them?" cried Caroline.

"Them!" said Beth.

"Students who are entering the parade singly, please stay in your classrooms until your room is called," came a voice over the loudspeaker. "Students who are part of a group costume, please line up in the hall."

"We'll worry about the boys later," said Beth. "Come on, Eddie, and help me bend this wire back into shape again. If we hurry we can fix up Izzie again before the parade starts."

"I'm going to fix *them*!" Eddie declared. "I don't know when or where, but they're not getting away with this. That's fighting dirty. They're so afraid we'll win the contest they can't stand it."

"We were ready to smash their pumpkins," Beth reminded her, and nobody spoke for a while. With the three of them working, it didn't take long to fix Izzie. Once they got their hands inside the chicken wire frame, they were able to shape the lizard the way it had been, and gradually the legs and head and body emerged, good as new.

But Caroline felt a part coming on, as actresses sometimes do. The alien spaceship had become a loathsome dragon, and only she, the fair and lovely maiden, could destroy it. While everyone waited in the hall for the parade to begin, she slipped out of her section of the chicken wire costume and into her empty classroom.

Opening her desk, she got out her new scissors, the best scissors she had ever had, scissors that had points as long and as sharp as an alligator's tooth. And then, aware of nothing else but the role she was destined to play, she walked down the line of costumes in the hall—past the troop of clowns, past the flowers in a pot, the swarm of bees, the deck of cards, the acrobats, until she saw the alien spaceship up ahead.

And then, the fair and lovely maiden faced the dragon, and, taking a deep breath, cast her eyes heavenward for courage. Holding the scissors in both hands over her head like a dagger, she ran forward and plunged the sharp points into the side of the giant inner tube, using all the strength she could muster.

BANG!

It was an explosion. Somehow Caroline had thought that the air would slowly leak out. Somehow she had thought it might be more like a soft hiss.

She fell backward, as Jake, Josh, Wally, and Peter stared down at the strip of black rubber that lay around their feet.

The next thing she knew, she was being led to the principal's office, Beth on one side of her for support, Eddie on the other, while the four Hatford brothers, still in shock, brought up the rear.

Twelve

Letters

What happened was that neither the Hatfords nor the Malloys won the contest. Both groups were disqualified because the boys had smashed the lizard to begin with, and Caroline had destroyed the spaceship.

Instead, five kids who were dressed up like instruments in a symphony orchestra won first place, and if *they* had been in on the bargain, both the Hatfords and Malloys would have been taking orders from a violin, a viola, a clarinet, a bassoon, and an oboe.

The girls had seemed almost relieved at the verdict. At least they didn't have to worry about being anyone's slaves, Wally thought. And maybe in a way he and his brothers were glad it was over, too, because they didn't want to be slaves, either, but they *had* had big plans for that inner tube on the river next summer. *That's* what hurt.

The boys stayed at school just long enough to drink some cider and eat some doughnuts at the Halloween party after the parade, but then they slipped away and headed home. It was the first Halloween they could remember that they had not been in the parade.

"This is absolutely, totally, all-out war," said Jake. "They ruined all the fun we could have had with that inner tube next summer, and for what? It didn't take them long to put their costume back together. We smashed it, but we didn't *destroy* it."

"We wanted to, though," Wally reminded him, but Jake paid no attention whatsoever.

"You know what I'd like to do to those girls? Trap them in the cemetery."

Wally looked quickly over at Jake as they slouched along the sidewalk toward home.

"*Then* what?" asked Wally.

"I don't know. That would probably be enough. They'd be scared out of their skin."

Would it never end? Wally wondered. When they were eighty-five-year-old men, would they still be trying to get even with three old women named Malloy? He could see it now: when Eddie, Beth, and Caroline each graduated from high school, the Hatford brothers would have to attend just so they could boo when a Malloy walked across the stage.

When each of the Malloy girls married, the Hatford brothers would go just so they could tie junk on the backs of their cars. Wherever the Malloy girls went, the Hatfords would forever follow just to make them miserable.

"Why don't we just forget them!" Wally said. "Tomorrow night's Halloween. Just forget them, and go trick-or-treating like we used to. If the Bensons were here, we'd be starting out about six o'clock, and we wouldn't stop till close to ten. We were always the first ones out on the street and the last ones in. Man, we'd get so much loot, we'd have enough candy to last all year."

"No matter what we do, we'll probably run into Beth or Caroline or Eddie," Jake said disgustedly. "They're *every*where!"

"They'll figure out some way to ruin Halloween for us," said Josh. "I wish we could just lock them up on Halloween night and have the town to ourselves."

"Fat chance," said Wally.

There was a letter waiting for them when they got home. It was a letter to Wally from his friend Bill Benson:

Dear Wally (and Josh and Jake and Peter):

We were making plans for Halloween the other day and wondered what you guys are doing this year. Man, we used to have fun, didn't we? Remember the time we soaped the windows of the principal's car? And the scavenger hunt in the cemetery? Remember the ghost-walk we had at our party when everyone was blindfolded and had to eat a spoonful of guts (spaghetti) and eyeballs (peeled grapes)?

I don't know whether we'll be going out trick-or-treating or not, because there are at least two parties going on. Maybe we'll go to both.

Tony's teacher (the "Georgia Peach") is going to come to school on Halloween dressed as a belly dancer. That's what she said, anyway. If she does, all us guys are going to be sitting in the first row, I know that. She probably won't, though.

Mom really likes it down here. She's got a part-time job in a bookstore, and I think she'd sort of like to stay. Dad doesn't know yet whether he wants to stay or not. Same with us. We really miss you guys, but Georgia's great too.

Anything happening there since we left? The Malloys taking good care of our house? They better not mess up the walls in our bedrooms with girl stuff.

Write when you can.

Bill (and Danny, Steve, Tony, and Doug)

Dear Bill (and Danny, Steve, Tony, and Doug):

Tomorrow's Halloween and you know how many parties we've been invited to? None. Zero. Today we were disqualified from the Halloween contest because we smashed the Malloys' chicken-wire lizard and flattened it like a pancake. It didn't make that much difference, because they got it back in shape by the time the parade began, but you know what Crazy Caroline did? Do you know how nuts she really is? Punctured our inner-tube spaceship with a pair of scissors. It exploded like a paper bag. Then they *got disqualified. Jake's up in his room trying to think of a way to get even. If you guys don't come back pretty soon, we are going to spend all our time thinking up ways to get even, and* they *are going to think up ways to get even, and if this goes on for a whole year, we'll go nuts.*

Don't fall in love with your teacher, even if she does *dress up like a belly dancer. Don't fall in love with Georgia either. Tell your mom she can get a job in the bookstore here.*

I mean it, you guys!

Wally (and Jake and Josh and Peter)

"I've got it!"

Jake came into Wally's room, where he was

just sealing his letter to Bill Benson. Josh and Peter followed him in, Peter still eating a peppermint patty he had found in his jeans pocket but had sat on, and it was as flat as a fifty-cent piece.

"What?" Wally asked.

"Something Bill said in his letter. About all the parties the guys were going to, and the scavenger hunt in the cemetery. Let's invite the girls to a party."

"Are you *nuts*?" cried Wally.

"No, let's invite them to a party. Just not *here*."

"What are you talking about?" asked Josh.

"We'll invite them to a party at some girl's house, but they'll have to go through the cemetery to get there."

Wally thought it over. "They'll never go."

"Sure they will. They can't resist."

"And then?" asked Josh.

"We'll think of something," Jake told him.

•

The boys spent the evening on the invitation. Jake and Josh even went to the drugstore and bought a pack of party invitations, half price, just for the one they wanted to use. It had to look official.

It was the kind girls would send, all right. There was a border all the way around of tiny pumpkins, and a perky little witch stirring a kettle of something. On the inside it said:

Little witch has come to say,
Ghosts and goblins like to play.
Won't you come and join the fun?
There'll be treats for everyone.
Time ________________________
Place ________________________

"Barf! Vomit!" said Jake, when he read it to Wally.

Wally studied the invitation. "But what are you going to write at the bottom?"

"That's what we have to figure out," said Jake. "Who do the girls run around with besides each other?"

"Caroline runs around with the girl who played the fairy godmother in the play," said Wally.

"Nope. Has to be in the same class as Eddie. If it's any younger, Beth and Eddie won't go. *Think,* Josh!" Jake said. "Who does Eddie hang around with?"

"What about the girl who plays shortstop at recess?"

"Mary Ruth?" said Jake.

"Yeah."

"Where does she live?" asked Wally.

Josh looked at Jake, and started to grin. "Over near the cemetery."

"Perfect!" said Jake.

The boys gathered around the dining-room table while Jake filled out the invitation with Mother's pen.

Time: *8 P.M. Halloween night (all-girl party)*
Place: *Mary Ruth Sayer's*
409 Bremer Road
P.S. *Meet at the north entrance to the cemetery, and bring a flashlight. Follow the clues.*

"What clues?" asked Peter.

"We'll have them posted all around the cemetery, right up to that bench by the stone wall in the Remembrance Garden," Jake told them. "When they get that far, we'll let them have it."

"Have what?" asked Peter.

"Worms," grinned Jake. "A bucket of worms. We'll be watching from the top of the wall, and as soon as they sit down, we dump."

Wally stared. "Do you know how long it takes to dig up a whole bucket of worms?"

"It will really be a bucket of spaghetti with a can of worms tossed in. There will be just enough worms wriggling about to make them think that it's all worms. They'll probably faint."

Peter sucked in his breath.

They spent the entire evening in Wally's room making a map of the cemetery and figuring out where to place the clues. Then, keeping the map for themselves, they put the invitation in its envelope and wrote, *Eddie, Beth, and Caroline* on the front. Just before going to bed Wally went across the swinging bridge beside Jake and Josh, and they silently dropped the envelope in the Malloys' mailbox.

Thirteen

Clues

"Girls," Mother said on Saturday, coming through the door with the mail in her hand, "it looks as though you got a party invitation. It's the right size, anyway."

Caroline, Beth, and Eddie were doing their Saturday chores. At the word *party* they all stopped their sweeping, dusting, and mopping and gathered around the small white envelope in Mother's hand.

"It didn't have a stamp, so someone must have hand-delivered it," Mother said, giving it to Eddie.

Eddie opened it up, and read aloud:

"Little witch has come to say,
Ghosts and goblins like to play.
Won't you come and join the fun?
There'll be treats for everyone."

"Yuk!" said Beth. "Who would send an invitation like that?"

Eddie stared at the name at the bottom. "It's Mary Ruth, from school! This doesn't sound like her."

"Maybe it's all she could find," said Mother. "Anyway, all three of you are invited."

Eddie kept reading. "It's tonight! The party starts at the cemetery and we have to follow clues. Now, that's more like it."

"And it's *all* girls!" said Beth.

"We won't even go trick-or-treating. We won't have to run into the boys," added Caroline.

"Maybe that's the way they do things here in West Virginia, deliver the invitation the day of the party," Mother said. "I think it's wonderful that you're making friends at school. Finish your work, and you can spend the rest of the day deciding on costumes."

The Malloy girls had always liked putting together their own costumes instead of buying them ready-made in the stores. Eddie decided to go as a football player, in one of Dad's old uniforms; Beth would go as a robot from outer space, with a stocking over her hair to make her look bald; and Caroline would wear her Goblin Queen costume from the play at school.

Caroline simply could not wait for the party to

begin, and when she heard Beth say that you went up one street to get to the cemetery, and Eddie saying no, you went up another, Caroline told them she would get on her bike and check it out.

It was almost five o'clock when Caroline left the house, and it was much colder then when they'd gone camping but still a beautiful October evening. Leaves fell down around her face and shoulders as she rode, and Caroline wondered if it ever got that beautiful in Ohio. Probably. She'd just never had as much fun back in Ohio as she did here, even though she *had* got herself and her sisters in trouble for stabbing the alien spaceship.

It wasn't all her fault, though. She never would have punctured their spaceship if they hadn't flattened Izzie. Why couldn't the Hatford boys be normal? Or was that normal for boys? She didn't know. Peter's only fault was that he was a Hatford. Wally might have turned out all right if he hadn't had Josh and Jake for brothers. It was the eleven-year-old twins she suspected of being the worst—Jake, for giving orders, and Josh, for the stuff he drew in his sketchbook.

She turned up a road at the edge of town. To the left of her were the gravestones of the Buckman cemetery—Eddie was right—and on up ahead she could see the big iron gate at the entrance. She began pedaling up the hill, but suddenly skidded to a stop, letting her bicycle tip, and fell over into a clump of weeds.

There, not thirty yards ahead, were Jake, Josh, and Wally, taping a piece of paper to the iron gate of the cemetery.

Them!

Caroline was torn between riding up to the boys and catching them in the act, or racing home to tell Beth and Eddie. She decided to stay put until the boys left, and as soon as they had gone through the gate and were out of sight, she pedaled home as fast as her feet would go.

She burst into the house and collapsed on the sofa, panting.

"Caroline?" said Beth, coming over.

Eddie clattered downstairs. "What's wrong?"

"Wait till you hear!" said Caroline, and told them that the boys had been taping something to the gate of the cemetery.

"Them!" cried Beth and Eddie together.

"I *wondered* why Mary Ruth didn't say anything in school yesterday about a party!" said Eddie. "Those dumb boys! Didn't they even think we might have called Mary Ruth to check it out?"

"But we didn't," Beth reminded her.

"You're right, we didn't. We almost fell for it. Well, there's only one thing to do. Go over to the cemetery now and see what they're up to."

They took a flashlight and headed up the street. When they got to the cemetery, there was the note the boys had taped to the gate: *Turn left and go to the first grave on the right.*

Beth and Caroline giggled. "They must think we're really stupid to fall for this," said Beth.

"But we would have if I hadn't seen them here," Caroline reminded her.

"Let's follow it and see what they were planning to do," said Eddie.

They soon found the tombstone, a stone pyramid, and there was a note taped to that: *Follow the winding drive to the fence.*

Cautiously the girls followed the winding drive, and when the beam of the flashlight fell on the fence, there, just as the instructions said, was another piece of paper: *Fifty steps to the right, then left to the shed.*

They found the shed. Still another note. *Follow the path on your left to the bench in the Remembrance Garden.*

"I don't like this," said Beth. "They're up to something, all right."

Quietly they followed the path until they came to a bench by a high stone wall, with rosebushes all around—probably a beautiful place in the summer, Caroline thought, but sinister-looking now in the moonlight.

Eddie shone the flashlight around. There was a note on the bench: *Sit here and wait for instructions,* it said.

"Oh, no, we don't," said Beth. "I'll bet it's wet paint." Gingerly she put out one hand and tested. Dry.

"They were probably going to jump out of the trees with masks on and scare us silly," said Caroline.

"Or throw water on us," said Beth. "Look how we'd have been trapped here in this corner, right up against the wall."

"Well, I think we ought to look around," said Eddie. They climbed the bank beside the wall, making their way through the bare rosebushes, until they had scrabbled to the top of the stone wall behind the bench.

"Eddie!" said Caroline. "Look here."

The girls stared at a pan sitting just behind the wall. It was an ordinary saucepan with a lid on it, as though someone had made a pot of stew and left it there to cool.

Slowly Caroline put out one hand and lifted the lid, as Eddie shone the light on it. "Spaghetti?" she said. And then she gave a little cry, because the spaghetti started to move.

"Worms!" gulped Beth.

"Spaghetti *and* worms!" said Eddie. "They

were going to *drop* them on us, I'll bet! They were going to be waiting right up there behind the wall, and as soon as we sat down on that bench, they were going to dump it on our heads!"

Caroline shivered with the thought. All three girls shivered.

"What are we going to do?" asked Beth.

"We are going to go home and leave the house again at five of eight, just as though we were going to a party," said Eddie. "Just in case they're watching. But after that . . ." She began to smile. "Trust me," she said, and took out a pen and paper.

Fourteen

Party

Jake, Josh, and Wally sat on the wall overlooking the bench in the Remembrance Garden, and watched for a beam of a flashlight that would tell them the girls were coming.

"I can't understand it," said Jake. "We saw them leave the house around eight, we followed them to the cemetery . . . we saw them start off with the first clue before we came over here. Where the heck could they be?"

"Peter was smart," said Josh. "He said he'd rather go trick-or-treating than get even with the girls. It's a good thing he didn't come. He'd never stop complaining."

"Well, you're doing a pretty good job of it yourself," grumbled Jake.

"Maybe they got lost and decided to go back," said Wally, feeling pretty cold and tired, too, and *certainly* ready to give up and go trick-or-treating. They had wasted enough time as it was.

"I don't think so. Eddie wouldn't give up that easily," Jake told him. "They were so close! There were only four clues altogether!"

"But *they* didn't know there were only four. Maybe they thought they'd be here all night," said Wally.

The boys sat huddled together another three or four minutes, scanning the dark cemetery for any sign of a light.

"Well, I don't know what happened to them, but this is a lousy way to spend Halloween," said Josh. "If we don't go trick-or-treating soon, people will start turning off their porch lights and we won't get anything. Peter's out there getting all the candy."

"Maybe he'll share it," said Jake.

"C'mon," said Wally. "I'm not going to wait a whole year for Halloween to come again."

"You guys give up too soon," said Jake. "They've *got* to come."

"Five more minutes, and then we go trick-or-treating," said Josh.

They waited. The wind picked up, and it grew colder still. And though Wally strained to see, there was no beam of light, no voices, no sound of leaves or footsteps, no snap of a twig.

"They've gone home," said Jake. "They *must* have gone home!"

"Or else they went over to Mary Ruth's and found out there wasn't any party," said Josh.

"Hoo boy, if *that* happened, they'll be ready to kill us," said Wally.

Jake jumped down off the wall. "Okay, I give up. Let's hit all the houses we can on the way back."

"You and your lousy ideas," grumbled Josh.

"You were in on it too!" Jake told him. "You helped choose the invitations. And you cooked the spaghetti, Wally, so don't blame it all on me."

"Don't remind me," said Wally. "What do we do with the spaghetti and worms?" He knelt down with the flashlight and lifted the lid on the saucepan. Then he gasped.

There was no spaghetti. No worms. Instead, there was a little piece of paper in the bottom of the pan, which read, *You boys come home this instant. Mom.*

Jake read it, then Josh.

"Oh, no! How did she find out!" said Josh.

"She must have missed her spaghetti. I *told* you we shouldn't have used the whole box, Jake!" Wally moaned.

"Are we ever going to catch it!" whistled Josh.

But Jake wasn't so sure. "Wait a minute," he said. "Think about it."

"I *am* thinking about it. We're in trouble," Wally croaked.

"Somehow this doesn't sound like Mom," Jake went on.

"Yes, it does," said Wally.

Jake shook his head. "Mom would say, 'You boys come home this *minute.*' Did you ever hear her say 'this *instant*'? And when she leaves us a note, she uses those little notepads from the hardware store, not a piece of yellow tablet paper. Also, she never prints, and *this* note is printed instead of written."

Wally looked at Josh, Josh looked at Jake.

"Them?" they cried.

"Them!" said Jake. "They're trying to ruin our Halloween. Somehow they found out what we were up to, and they figure we'll go right home, confess everything, and lose out on trick or treats."

Wally felt an enormous burden lifting off his chest. "Then we *don't* have to go straight home?"

"Of course not. Somebody's got to carry the pan, but there's still time to hit a lot of houses."

Wally carried the pan. They headed for the cemetery entrance, and the first row of houses just beyond.

"Where are your costumes?" one woman

asked them. "You boys don't look like trick-or-treaters to me." But she gave them candy anyway.

The pickings were slim, however. Some people had already turned off their lights. Some houses had run out of candy, and still others were down to little boxes of raisins or pennies. The dentist was even giving out apples instead of candy!

Desperate, they fanned out, trying to ring as many doorbells as possible. Sometimes, Wally knew, when you were the last one to come by, people dropped all the remaining candy in your bag, but it wasn't happening now, and he had to work twice as hard and run twice as fast to fill up even his pockets.

They met again on the corner, and by twenty after nine there were no more porch lights on anywhere. A policeman cruising by stopped when he saw them and rolled down his window. "You fellas better get on home now," he called.

Silently, glumly, Jake and Josh and Wally turned toward home, with barely enough candy to carry in their jackets. Mother always said that Halloween candy should last all year, and they'd hardly picked up enough to last through December.

"You know what I'm thinking?" Jake said as they turned up their street. "Maybe it's time we called a truce. I mean, just give up bugging the girls. *Forget* about them. Find other guys at school to hang around with. Whether the Malloys stay here or not probably doesn't have anything to do with what the Bensons decide. Those girls have ruined enough things for us. This Halloween was really the pits."

"I've been trying to *tell* you that," said Wally. "I'm getting a little tired of 'The Malloys this . . .' and 'The Malloys that. . . .' Everything we do, practically, is connected to the Malloys."

"Okay," said Jake. "As of right now, we just forget about them. They can go, they can stay, it doesn't make any difference to us."

"I feel better already," said Wally, with a sigh.

"So do I," said Josh.

They went up the steps to the house.

"We should have done this long ago," said Jake. "We're free! Back to boy-stuff again." He smiled. Josh smiled. Wally smiled. They opened the door.

There in the living room sat Eddie, Beth, and Caroline in their costumes, as well as Peter in his pajamas, a ring of chocolate around his mouth.

Mrs. Hatford hurried toward the boys. "Where in the world have you been?" she asked, and for a minute Wally thought she was going to sail right past them and on out the door. "Why did you invite these girls to a party and then not even have the decency to show up? You didn't even *mention* it to me."

"A party?" cried Jake and Josh and Wally together.

But before they could say another word, the girls all chanted together:

"Little witch has come to say,
Ghosts and goblins like to play.
Won't you come and join the fun?
There'll be treats for everyone."

"Jake, I want you to take your money and run to the store for some Cokes or something. Josh, you're in charge of games," Mrs. Hatford said.

And as Wally watched helplessly, his mother took all the candy they had collected, dumped it in a bowl, and passed it around the room for starters.

WHOSE SIDE ARE YOU ON?

The Hatford Boys
or
The Malloy Girls

Send us your vote!
Write BOYS or GIRLS on a piece of paper or a postcard.
Be sure to include your name, address, and age.
Mail your vote to:

THE BOYS VS. THE GIRLS VOTE
Bantam Doubleday Dell BFYR
1540 Broadway
New York, NY 10036

Mail your vote by May 1, 1995. Your name will be entered in a random drawing where you can win 5 autographed books by Phyllis Reynolds Naylor for yourself and 5 for your school!

OFFICIAL CONTEST RULES

NO PURCHASE NECESSARY TO ENTER OR RECEIVE THE PRIZE. To enter, write your name, address, and age on a piece of paper or a postcard. Mail your entry to: THE BOYS VS. THE GIRLS VOTE, Bantam Doubleday Dell BFYR, 1540 Broadway, New York, NY 10036. Limit one entry per person. All entries must be received by May 1, 1995. The winner will be notified by September 1, 1995.

Employees of Bantam Doubleday Dell Publishing Group, Inc. and its affiliates and subsidiaries and their immediate family members are not eligible. Void where prohibited or restricted by law.